## From the Files of

# Madison Finn

## All Shook Up

By Laura Dower

HYPERION
New York

For all the fans,
who shake me up (in a good way)

Text copyright © 2006 by Laura Dower

*From the Files of Madison Finn* is a trademark of Disney Enterprises, Inc.

Printed in the United States of America

First Edition
1 3 5 7 9 10 8 6 4 2

The main body of text of this book is set in 11.5-point Frutiger Roman.

ISBN 0-7868-3779-9

Visit www.hyperionbooksforchildren.com

# Chapter 1

From her seat in Mr. Gibbons's English classroom, Madison had a clear view of the school parking lot, a stretch of winding road that ran alongside Far Hills Junior High. More than anything, Madison wanted to race down that road for home.

But she was stuck inside English class. The students listened to Roger Willoughby, one of the smarter kids in class, as he presented a speech about himself. Roger had not only described his carrot-orange hair perfectly, but he'd slipped in a few jokes about his lisp, his bad handwriting, and his ability to perform magic tricks.

The class was in hysterics. He was a hit.

Madison's mind, however, was elsewhere. Her gaze

drifted from tree to tree outside the window as she silently considered how she could possibly give a speech without putting the entire class to sleep. She wrote in her files all the time, so it wasn't as if she were a terrible writer or anything, but right now, hearing Roger's jokes made her doubt her own speech-writing skills.

Whenever Madison thought too hard about something, her mind got all knotted up.

This was one of those times.

After Roger finished, everyone clapped politely, including Madison.

Hart Jones was next.

Hart was a great distraction for Madison; and for a fleeting moment, her doubts faded. Her eyes took in his perfect blue sweater and even more perfect faded blue jeans. His hair, his eyes, his mouth—*everything* about Hart seemed perfectly perfect.

Lately, Hart had moved from being Madison's crush to being a very real deal. Everyone at school knew, or at least Madison's friends all knew, that the pair had graduated to couple status. They'd actually held hands three times already: once at the movies, once on Madison's front porch, and once in school—although just for five seconds, in the hallway. They had not done anything more than that, but Madison was one hundred percent certain that Hart was destined to be the great love of her life. Well, at least the great love of her seventh-grade life.

Hart's speech mentioned hockey and mystery

books by R. L. Stine and Eoin Colfer. He talked about his family vacations every year; building a log cabin with his father; and the summer his pet dog Bingo died. Hearing about any dog dying made Madison feel a little sad; but knowing Hart had lost *his* dog made Madison feel sadder than sad. She wondered if that were why he didn't have a pet right now.

When Hart finished, the class applauded again. Madison's heart began to race.

Her turn was coming closer.

Madison glanced out the window again and sighed, trying to remember the details of her speech that she had tried to memorize at home the night before. She sneaked a peek at story notes placed on the desk in front of her. Her brain felt fuzzy.

Meanwhile, another girl—a stranger, really—began to read. Madison had often stared at the back of the girl's head during class, but they had never spoken. All Madison knew was that the girl's name was Madhur. It seemed impossible that two class-mates could sit in a classroom together for so long and not know one another. But they had never had a reason to interact.

Until now.

Madhur had long black hair wound up tightly in a snug tortoiseshell clip; it looked shimmery blue-black in sunlight. She spoke in a low voice with a light accent.

"My parents speak Punjabi at home," Madhur

said, quickly stringing words together like colored beads on a thread. "And then of course they also speak Hindi. And Urdu. And English sometimes . . . well . . . obviously. I mean, my mom wants me to learn as many languages as possible, but especially our family's dialect. I was born here, but my grand-mamma always tells me about Punjab, and I know I want to keep that place in my heart for always."

Madison pricked up her ears when she heard the word "Punjab," because she remembered a time when her own mom had flown over to Pakistan and India for a work-related project. She couldn't believe that Madhur's family was from a part of the world so far away.

"The Punjab state animal is the buck, also called *kala hiran*," Madhur continued. "It has a black coat and spiral horns. When I was a little girl, my grand-mamma got me a stuffed animal that looked just like it. Of course, I love animals."

Madison found herself grinning when she heard that part, because of course, she loved animals, too. She and Madhur had some important things in common.

"Punjab is a part of the world that is rich with culture. I believe that knowing about my family history makes me a wiser person."

Mr. Gibbons looked very pleased—and proud—as he listened to Madhur's speech. His brown eyes did not stray from Madhur the entire time she read aloud. Neither did Madison's, nor anyone else's. Madhur had locked on to everyone's gaze with some kind of invisible tractor beam.

"Grandmamma tells me stories about Punjabi thunderstorms. She always says the thunderstorms in the countryside deliver lightning that splits the sky into pieces."

Madison's mind lurched at that description. She imagined a blue sky cut apart like a puzzle.

"In many places, when the temperature has been so hot for so long, a thunderstorm is like the greatest gift. I like to think of the rain like that, like a gift for everyone in its path. Birds like mynahs and black hummingbirds dance on the telephone wires and trees. Of course, rain soon becomes the monsoon. Even though I have never seen one, never seen the sky turn dark like ink, I feel like I've experienced all of it. Punjab is a part of me, just like Far Hills is a part of me."

The class let out a collective sigh as Madhur finished up. Almost without being aware of it, Madison began clapping enthusiastically. She couldn't believe what a good writer Madhur was. How could one of her classmates have written such a beautiful and poetic story for a homework assignment?

When Mr. Gibbons and the other students joined in the clapping, Madison saw Madhur's head dip down a little bit. Was she embarrassed by the attention?

"Okay, Madison Finn, you're up," Mr. Gibbons said.

Madison shot him a look. "Huh?"

"Your turn to speak," Mr. Gibbons said.

"S—s—speak?" Madison stuttered.

A few of her classmates chuckled.

"Oh," Madison said, recovering. "Of course. My speech." She looked down at her notes.

```
film locations
Amazon forest
editing
cutting-room floor
Mom
great experience
computers
keep track
first plane ride to nowhere
London
South America
my files
```

The door to the classroom was ajar, and for a split second, Madison thought about running out of the room. She could make a clean getaway if she bolted right now . . . Madison's hands felt all clammy and started to shake. Her voice wavered. She looked over at Madhur for encouragement; and Madhur gave her a wide smile.

Concentrate! Madison thought. Breathe!

Before she could get another word out, the final bell rang.

"I'm sorry that we've run out of time, Madison," Mr. Gibbons said. "Why don't we finish up next class?"

Madison had never been so grateful to hear a bell. "No problem," she told the teacher.

As students filed out of class, Mr. Gibbons wrote on the board in big letters: DON'T FORGET! JUNIOR WORLD LEADERS CONFERENCE IN LESS THAN TWO WEEKS!

He underlined "two."

"I just want to remind everyone who already signed up to assist at the conference that there's an important meeting tomorrow. And for those of you who have not yet signed up, it's not too late! This is the first time Far Hills has ever hosted a weekend event like this. It should not be missed!"

Madison and her friends had signed up a week earlier. The middle-school conference would feature panel discussions about important issues like hunger, AIDS, poverty, terrorism, and more. It seemed so exciting! One of Madison's BFFs, Fiona Waters, had even been chosen as a speaker for the event. Unlike Madison, who preferred working *behind* the scenes, Fiona loved being center stage. Madison's other longtime BFF, Aimee Gillespie, also loved the spotlight. Aimee was a ballet dancer who loved performing. Sometimes Madison wondered how people so different from her could turn into her best friends ever.

Everybody shuffled toward the door of the

classroom. There were a few moments left before the next bell. Madison grabbed her bag and pushed toward the door along with everyone else. Madhur was already out in the hall.

Madison wanted to tell Madhur how much the presentation about Punjab had meant to her. And she had questions, too. But a crowd of kids was in the way, and Madhur seemed too far to reach.

"Wait! Finnster!"

Hearing her name, Madison turned around and collided with Hart. As they bumped, Madison felt Hart's hand press into the small of her back.

"Hey," he mumbled. "Great job on your presentation."

"Really?" Madison asked.

"Really."

Madison smiled. "Thanks."

Hart's hand moved away from her back. Now he touched her shoulder.

"You going to Math?" he asked.

"Math?"

Madison caught a glimpse of Madhur out of the corner of her eye. She started to follow Madhur toward the next class.

"Where are we going?" Hart asked, sticking close to Madison as they walked down the hallway.

A cluster of their friends—Walter "Egg" Diaz; Drew Maxwell; Dan Ginsburg; and Fiona's brother, Chet—appeared from around a corner.

Madison sighed. Her eyes darted around the hall-way again, but Madhur was gone.

"Who you looking for?" Egg asked in his typical, obnoxious voice.

"No one," Madison shrugged.

"The bogey man?" Dan joked.

"Or the booger man," Chet said, cracking up at his own lame joke.

Madison rolled her eyes. "No one, really," Madison insisted. "Just this girl from class."

"Who?" Hart asked.

"That girl Madhur," Madison said. "She did such a great presentation, and I just wanted to tell her how much I loved it."

"I know Madhur. She's cool," Chet said.

"Huh?" Madison replied. Chet never said any girl was cool.

"She's smart, too," Chet added.

Just then Egg, Drew, and Dan started a shoving match in the hallway. They weren't listening. The second bell was about to ring.

"How do you know Madhur?" Madison asked Chet.

"Duh," Chet said. "She's in our grade."

"Oh, I know *that*," Madison said. "But . . ."

"Race you guys to Math," Drew cried. All the boys dashed away, leaving Madison standing solo in the middle of the hallway.

"Later, Finnster!" Hart called back before disap-pearing with the rest of the group.

Madison slung her bag over her shoulder. She couldn't believe that after all that time in seventh grade with her friends and classmates she had failed to notice someone as interesting as Madhur.

*Rrrrrrrrrrrrrrrrrring!*

The bell! Quickly, Madison tripped down the hall toward Math, feet—and mind—racing.

# Chapter 2

After math class, Madison headed for lunch. She still had Madhur on the brain—big-time.

Madison didn't remember ever having seen Madhur in line for food or sitting at a table in the cafeteria. But today, there she was. It reminded Madison of something Gramma Helen always said, about how funny it was to learn a new word, because as soon as you did, that word appeared *everywhere*.

Madison jumped in line behind Madhur. "Hey," she said loudly.

Madhur whirled around, clutching her chest.

"Whoa! You scared me," Madhur said. "I was spacing out on the macaroni and cheese. It looks especially disgusting today."

Madison smiled. "I'm sorry to come over like this. . . . I mean, we've never talked before. . . . You don't really know me. . . ."

"Sure I know you. You're Madison Finn." Madhur said matter-of-factly.

Madison was taken aback. "Yeah, that's me."

"You did a fab job today on your speech in English," Madhur said, her voice sounding as cheery as it had earlier that day. "Until class had to be dismissed, that is."

Madison was caught off guard by Madhur's compliment. "That's what I was going to say to you just now. . . ."

"What?"

"I wanted to tell *you* how much I liked *your* story . . . about Punjab . . . and your parents . . . and your culture . . ."

"Oh. Thanks," Madhur said.

By now they had moved to the front of the food line. Fiona, Aimee, and their other friend, Lindsay Frost, pounced on Madison when they saw her.

"Where have you *beeeeeen*?" Aimee wailed. She took Madison by the arm.

"We've been waiting for ten minutes," Lindsay said, even though Madison knew she was (of course) exaggerating.

"Maddie," Fiona said to Madhur. "Meet us at the table."

Madison smiled. "I'm sorry, Madhur. My friends . . ."

"No biggie," Madhur said, filling her lunch tray.

Madison followed. "I really wanted you to know how much you totally inspired me today," she said. "I'm a writer, too, or at least I want to be a writer sometimes. . . ."

"That's cool," Madhur said, chuckling. She popped a french fry into her mouth and chewed. "Hey, are you going to eat now? You wanna sit together?"

Madison grinned. By now, Fiona and the others had moved through the salad bar and were headed toward the usual orange table at the back of the cafeteria.

"My friends and I usually sit . . . there. . . ." Madison said, pointing. "You can sit with us if you want."

Madhur shrugged, lifting her tray. "Why not?"

As they walked toward the orange table, Madison heard someone call out her name. It was Ivy Daly, Madison's mortal enemy. She sat alongside her drones, Rose and Joan.

"Hello-o-o-o-o, Madison," Ivy said snidely. "Um, do you have the science notes? I don't have mine, and I think Mr. Danehy's giving a quiz today."

"He *is* giving a quiz," Madison said, "and my notebook is in my locker."

"Can you get it for me?" Ivy asked.

Rose, aka Rose Thorn, snickered.

"Get it for you? I don't think so," Madison said. "See you in class."

"Wait!"

Ivy dashed over and put her arm on Madison as if Madison were her best friend in the universe, squeezing just a little bit too hard.

"Please, Maddie," Ivy said. "I just need to look at the notes during my study period, and then I'll give them right back, I swear. Pretty please with chocolate chips and whipped cream on top?"

Madison sighed. "Just one class period?"

"I swear. Cross my heart," Ivy said, smirking.

"Fine," Madison moaned, giving in.

Before walking away, Ivy shot a look at Madhur as if to say, *Who are* you?

Madhur caught the look. She leaned in to Madison as they walked on.

"You're friends with *her*?" Madhur asked.

"Well," Madison explained, "not exactly friends."

"Because Ivy Daly is just so-o-o-o not like you. I mean, for one thing, she's super stuck-up. And her friends are even worse. One time they said some pretty mean things to me in the girls' bathroom."

"Yeah, they can be cold," Madison said.

"*Icebergs* is more like it," Madhur said in her slight accent. "Brrrrr."

Madison giggled. "We call her Poison Ivy."

"Poison Ivy?" Madhur cried. "Perfect! She's like an itch you can't scratch."

14

They both laughed out loud.

Hart waved Madison over to the orange table. He was saving an empty space on the bench just for her. He'd been saving her seats at lunch for weeks.

"What's up, Finnster?" Hart asked.

Madison dragged Madhur over. "I think there's enough room for two of us," she said, sitting down.

Of course there *wasn't* enough room for both of them. Aimee had to move over. Lindsay stood up and sat back down again. Hart had to shift over. Egg had to complain—as usual. Fiona was pleased with the seating reorganization, however. All the moving around pushed Egg that much closer to her new seat.

Madison noticed Aimee staring at Madhur; and she knew what the stares were all about. Aimee was extremely territorial when it came to lunchroom seating—and friends.

"Thanks for letting me sit here," Madhur said. "The cafeteria looks different from this table."

"I liked your talk in class," Hart said to Madhur. "You're a good writer."

Madhur nodded. "You are, too," she said, looking away from Hart.

Across the table, Egg flicked one of his fries. It landed in Madison's lap.

"Thanks a lot, moron," Madison said. "What am I supposed to do with this?"

"Stick it in your nose," Egg said.

"You're so funny I forgot to laugh."

"You forgot to barf?" Egg cracked.

The other boys laughed loudly.

"*You* make me want to barf," Madison said.

Madhur giggled. "You and Walter must be good friends," she whispered.

"Yeah, this whole group has all known each other forever," Madison explained. "Everyone except Fiona and Chet. They just moved here last summer from California."

"I know them," Madhur said, glancing over in Chet's direction. "Fiona seems nice. So does her brother."

"Before, when I was telling you about how much I liked your presentation," Madison said, "I forgot to tell you that I know a little bit about Punjabi culture."

"Really? How?"

Madison shrugged. "It's my mom, actually. She's a documentary filmmaker and producer, and she's been to Pakistan and India. She told me all about the monsoons. And her crew took this incredible footage, too. The way you described the weather and the places was so intense."

"Just my grandmamma's words," Madhur interrupted. "I've actually never been."

"Well, I felt like I really understood what you were saying," Madison said. "I think I'm going to surf the Net and find out more information about that part of the world."

Madhur ate a bite of salad from her plate. "Do you go online very much?" she asked Madison.

Aimee, who happened to overhear Madhur's question, laughed out loud.

"Did you just ask Madison if she ever went online?"

"Is that a funny question?" Madhur asked, sounding confused.

"My friends tease me," Madison said. "The truth is I'm on the computer most of the time. I keep these files, I have a screen name at bigfishbowl.com, I have a long-distance keypal . . . the works."

"I've heard of bigfishbowl. I've never been on it, though."

"You've never been?" Madison said.

"Wow," Fiona said. "You're missing out."

Lindsay grinned. "We gossip . . . well, chat . . . online all the time there."

"I don't actually have a computer at home that works. I go to the library to check my e-mail or do homework," Madhur explained.

"You don't have a computer at home?" Madison asked, incredulously.

Madhur shook her head. "My dad said maybe this year we will get one." .

Madison felt guilty. Not only did she have her very own personal computer—it was right there in her orange messenger bag.

"Maybe you should help on the school Web site,"

Madison suggested to Madhur. "Then you could use Mrs. Wing's computers to do work."

"That's a good idea," Madhur said. "I'm trying to do more extracurricular activities, rather than just studying all the time."

"Do you play sports?" Fiona asked. "You should join the soccer team."

"No way. I'm a total klutz," Madhur said. "I tried soccer once, and I tripped on the ball."

"Everyone trips on the ball!" Fiona said.

"Well . . ."

"It's not like you have to dance ballet or something," Fiona joked, eyeing Aimee. "Soccer is all practice and kicking and—I'm sure you'd have fun."

"I bet you'd be good at soccer," Chet blurted out from across the table.

The girls all stared.

Normally, Chet didn't pay attention to anything girls said or did. But today he was acting differently.

"Who asked you?" Fiona grumbled, kicking Chet under the table.

"It's a free country," Chet barked. "I can talk if I want to. . . ."

Fiona pounded him in the shoulder.

*"Settle down! Settle down!"* Dan said, imitating Principal Bernard's voice.

Lindsay laughed.

Madhur stood up all of a sudden. She seemed unfazed by the whole exchange. "I'm going back to get one of those giant brownies I saw. Does anyone want anything?"

"I'll take a brownie," Dan said.

"I'd love an orange," Fiona said sweetly.

"Can you grab me some chocolate milk?" Lindsay asked.

"You bet," Madhur said. "What about you, Maddie?"

"I don't need anything else," Madison said. "Thanks for asking."

As Madhur walked back toward the kitchen, Hart leaned in to Madison. "What's up with Madhur?" he asked. "Did she invite herself over to our table, or what?"

"I invited her," Madison said.

"Why?" Aimee said, sounding a little Ivy-like.

"Because," Madison said. "I wanted to."

"She's sweet," Fiona said, shooting another look at her brother. "Don't you think so, Chet?"

"What are you looking at *me* for?" Chet stammered.

Madison giggled. She wasn't the only person at the table who thought Madhur was cool. It was probably the first time she and Chet had ever agreed on anything.

"You should have heard her in English class today," Madison went on. "She has such an interesting life."

"Oh, yeah?" Fiona asked.

"Her family speaks, like, five languages," Madison said.

"Whatever," Aimee said, rolling her eyes.

The boys stood up with their emptied trays and moved away from the orange table.

Aimee stood up, too.

"Why are you acting like that?" Madison asked.

"Like what?" Aimee replied.

"That. You know."

"No, I don't," Aimee said firmly.

"You always do this," Madison said. "Whenever I make a new friend, you get weird."

"I do not."

Madison sighed.

"Remember when Fiona first moved here?" Madison asked Aimee.

Aimee shrugged. "Okay, fine. I acted a little weird. But only because you're my best friend. That's all. You can only have so many best friends, Madison."

"Who made that rule?" Madison asked.

Aimee didn't respond. She tried to change the subject.

"So, what's going on with Hart today?" Aimee asked. "He's so into you. Did you see the way he saved you a seat?"

"Aim!" Madison cried.

Fiona laughed, so Madison had to laugh, too.

"What's so funny?" Madhur said reappearing with the brownie, orange, and chocolate milk.

"Private joke," Aimee said.

Madison was a little taken aback by Aimee's curt response, but she tried to gloss over it.

"Hey, Madhur, do you have study period next?" Madison asked. "Because if you do, I was thinking of heading up to the media room in the library to do a little work. I could show you bigfishbowl. . . ."

"I can't," Madhur said, taking a big bite of brownie; she chewed and talked at the same time. "I have to meet with Mr. Gibbons. I'm working on the conference that's coming up in two weeks. . . ."

"You signed up?" Madison asked. "So did we."

"That's great," Madhur said. "So we're all in it together."

"Great," Aimee said, rather unenthusiastically.

As the lunch bell rang, the conversation came to a screeching halt. Poison Ivy swooped in.

"So, lunch is over. Are you going to your locker now?" Ivy asked. "Because you promised me that notebook. . . ."

Madison saw both Madhur and Aimee out of the corner of her eye. The two of them made the exact same "How can you possibly be talking to *her*?" face.

"The notebook," Madison repeated. "Right."

Madison gave her friends—including Madhur— a quick wave good-bye and headed into the hallway with her enemy. They walked down the hallway toward the stairs and over to Madison's bank of lockers.

"I can't believe you're hanging out with that geek," Ivy said to Madison.

"Who?" Madison asked.

"Madhur Singh, of course," Ivy said. "She is so dramatically, terribly uncool."

"What are you talking about?" Madison asked. "She *is* cool."

"You must be joking. She has no sense of style."

"And you do?" Madison said.

"You are kidding, right?" Ivy said.

"Here," Madison said firmly as she pressed a tattered science notebook into Ivy's hands.

"It's about time," Ivy said.

Madison sighed and headed off to the study hall. She found a comfortable seat in the back and logged on to a library computer. Her laptop battery was running low, and she'd forgotten to recharge.

Reaching into her bag, Madison pulled out a pen. Naturally, the cap was off. Just my luck, Madison thought. The entire vessel of ink spurted onto her favorite sky-blue, collared T-shirt. She looked as though she'd been attacked by a squid.

"My, my, what happened to you?" someone said from behind one of the stacks.

It was Mr. Books, the librarian.

"Pen catastrophe," Madison said, trying to look chipper.

"Never fight a pen," Mr. Books said. "The pen will always win."

Madison knew she should laugh, but she just didn't think the joke was funny. She'd been splattered! What was funny about *that*?

"Are you signed up for that conference at the school next week?" Mr. Books asked Madison.

"In two weeks," Madison corrected him. "Yeah, I signed up."

"I'll be running the projectors," Mr. Books said. "It's going to be a doozy of a day. Good for you for participating. All of Far Hills Junior High's best and brightest will be there."

"Thanks," Madison said awkwardly. It often felt more awkward but somehow more satisfying when a teacher (or, in this case, a librarian) gave her a compliment. Usually Mr. Books was growling or chasing the kids out of the library for talking too much, and Madison tried to avoid him wherever possible.

But today, Mr. Books was actually being friendly.

He walked away with a smile on his face, and Madison couldn't help thinking that there was something strangely significant about that moment.

Something big *was* about to happen.

Madison just couldn't put her finger on what it was.

# Chapter 3

By the time Madison returned home from school, her brain was whizzing with all of the things she had to do. First, there was math and reading homework. Then there was Internet research on Punjab—just to impress Madhur. Then she needed to log on to bigfishbowl to check e-mails, and then she had to see if anyone had posted something interesting on The Wall. After that, she needed to—

Madison stopped short on her porch. A note was taped to the door.

Maddie,
 Had to dash into the city for a MAJOR meeting with another film co. This is a really big deal, honey bear.

*Dad is picking you up for dinner. Told him to call you after 4. Sorry for the short notice! Use your spare key to get inside. Phin is down the street w/ Blossom + the Gillespies, so you don't have to worry about him.*

*Love,*
*Mom*

Madison dropped her orange messenger bag on the porch and sat down. Mom had to work *again*? Outside, the sky began to darken, and there was a chill in the air. She fished around in the pocket of her bag for the spare house key. It wasn't there; it wasn't wedged in between two books; it wasn't any-where! Even after Madison had dumped out the entire contents of the bag, including her laptop computer, a collection of Hello Kitty! pencils, a half-eaten granola bar, a package of pink-polka-dotted tissues, a stick of gum, several pennies, and her math textbook, she still had not located the key.

She didn't even have the sound of Phin barking at the front door to comfort her. Madison was all alone out there.

Just then she remembered where her spare key was—upstairs on her dresser. She'd left it there by mistake when she last cleaned out her bag.

"But there's another one!" Madison said aloud.

She remembered the *spare*, spare key Mom hid in the garden.

She scrambled to her feet and went over to the windowsill. A row of violets in yellow ceramic pots sat there. Madison lifted each pot, one by one.

*Dirt. Pebbles. No key?*

What was Madison supposed to do now? She briefly entertained the idea of running next door to her neighbor Josh's house. She had a little crush on Josh, a ninth grader from FHJH, and he was always very nice to Madison.

But on second thought, Madison decided that facing him would be too embarrassing. So she stayed where she was on the porch. She'd wait there until Dad showed up. It was a little after three o'clock. Madison could wait for an hour, couldn't she?

Madison crossed the porch to the wicker sofa and took a seat, placing her laptop in her lap. Luckily, her battery was fully charged and her wireless connection working, since she *was* practically inside the house. As she curled up in a ball and logged on to bigfishbowl, Madison heard the familiar *ding!* telling her there was mail in her e-mailbox.

| FROM | SUBJECT |
|------|---------|
| ✉ GoGramma | Thank you, dear |
| ✉ Dantheman | Clinic R.I.P. |
| ✉ BoopDeeDop | Account Info Please |
| ✉ Rainbowz Inc. | Make Money FA$T |
| ✉ Bigwheels | Where have u been??? |

26

Madison clicked on the e-mail from Gramma Helen. She knew it was a note of thanks for Madison's homemade card and gift.

She was right.

```
From: GoGramma
To: MadFinn
Subject: Thank you, dear
Date: Wed 23 Sept 12:12 PM
```
My dearest Madison,

I opened my mailbox this morning and found your lovely package. I was flat-out floored, my dear. You outdid yourself for my birthday this year. I particularly loved the copy of the photograph you found showing me and your grandpa together on our honeymoon. Wherever did you find that one? Needless to say, I ran right over to the framer. It will hang in my front hallway and I will think of you every time I see it. I am getting choked up just now thinking of it. You are a love. What is the e-mail chat symbol for happy tears?

Love,

Gramma

Madison e-mailed Gramma Helen right away with the symbol she was looking for.

:~ . . . )

Next, she opened the e-mail from Dan Ginsburg. He'd sent it from the animal clinic where Madison and he volunteered. Madison sensed right away that it was bad news.

From: DantheMan
To: MadFinn
Subject: Clinic R.I.P.
Date: Wed 23 Sept 2:33 PM
Maddie I got here after school b/c my mom called me and I have REALLY bad news 4 u. REALLY Bad.

Those kittens we brought in last week, the ones that were really sick, well all of them died except for one and Dr. Wing says he's not doing good at all. I am so so bummed out. I thought we might even keep one and I know u wanted to ask ur mom 2 keep one 2.

I guess they had some kind of infection b4 they were even brought in here, that's what doc says. So,

I was hoping maybe u would come in 2 help me 2morrow b/c I wanna bury them out back. Can u? Lemmeknow @ school. Bye.

Now Madison really wanted to cry. Not only was she locked out of her house, but Gramma Helen had gotten all e-mushy on her, and now Dan had this terrible news. Everything felt all shook up.

Madison sent Dan an instant reply. She told him she would come to the clinic to help out. She owed the clinic a volunteer visit anyway. It had been more than a week since Madison had been in to clean cages or help feed the animals or even help Dan's mom, Eileen, organize files in the front office. Madison did all sorts of odd jobs when she was there—anything to be a little bit closer to the animals she loved so much.

Overhead, the sky boomed with a clap of thunder, and the sky appeared to darken even more. Madison knew the rain was coming now for sure. It was nearly three thirty. Thankfully, Dad would be there soon to pick her up. Madison thought she heard a phone ringing inside, but she couldn't know whether it was Dad. She figured he would just come over when she didn't pick up. Dad was smart about that kind of stuff. Wasn't he?

She turned her attention back to the laptop.

The next e-mail looked familiar; a promotion

from Madison's favorite online store, Boop Dee Doop. She opened it to find an odd note from the store manager asking Madison to provide her personal and credit information, because it had been lost during a computer upgrade. Madison paused to examine the note more closely. Something about it seemed funny. Upon closer examination, Madison realized that the e-mail wasn't from the store at all. The address was different—off by one letter. She quickly hit DELETE. She deleted the next e-mail, too. Nothing more than spam. It was a good thing that Dad had taught Madison to be such a careful e-mailer.

Fortunately, the last e-mail in the mailbox was A-OK. Madison grinned as it opened up on-screen.

From: Bigwheels
To: MadFinn
Subject: Where have u been???
Date: Wed 23 Sept 2:58 PM

I am so bored that my brain has cobwebs--I swear. I am sitting here in the media lab @ school waiting for my teacher to come over & look @ our assignments that I finished 10 million hours ago. Ugh. Sometimes tech class is so cool and other times people r sooooo slow and I am . . . well, cobwebby, like I said.

But enuf about MOI how R U??? How
is the HART MAN? LOL That sounds
kind of like Bart Man on the
Simpsons, doesn't it?

I have cool newz, which is that my
school decided @ the last minute to
host this history conference and I
am going to be 1 of 7 presenters 4
the middle schoolers. Cool right???
I think so. My mom and dad told me
they were so proud that they might
even buy me an iPod. I told them
that was totally materialistic and
I couldn't accept.

LOL!!!! Of course I will accept it
if they give it. Wouldn't u? I'll
tell u more about the conference
when I find out more. Right now I'm
kinda in the dark.

OK the teacher's coming. Gotta dash.

Yours till the iPods (of course!!!),

Vicki aka Bigwheels

p.s.: I almost 4got to tell u that
I got this really cool new feature
on my e-mail that lets me attach

pics and little videos. I hope I
can send u something soon.

Bye.

The sky rumbled again. Like Bigwheels, Madison
felt kind of in the dark herself.
*Ding! Ding!*
The e-mailbox beeped again. She glanced down.
A brand-new e-mail flashed. She opened it.

From: JeffFinn
To: MadFinn
Subject: <no subject>
Date: Wed 23 Sept 4:03 PM
Honey I got an urgent message from
your mother and I tried calling the
house but I can't get you. Where
are you? Oh, honey, I am not even
in Far Hills right now--I had to
catch an afternoon flight out and
I'm sitting on the runway at Logan
Airport in Boston. And Stephanie is
away in D.C. on a sales call.


I just called over to Aimee's house
and her mom says you should go over
there as soon as you get this. I am
SO sorry, honey. Call me when you
get this. I will keep trying the

house, too. I hope you aren't sitting
out on the porch waiting for me.

Love you,

Dad

Madison stared dumbly at the computer screen.
Dad wasn't even in Far Hills right now?
Of course it wasn't really a problem, Dad being in
Boston. Aimee lived just a few houses down, and
Phinnie was already there, and Madison was just fine
on her own like this. After all, she was practically
thirteen. Well, twelve and three-quarters, anyhow.
She was old enough. She was responsible enough.
Madison hit a quick REPLY.

From: MadFinn
To: JeffFinn
Subject: Re: <no subject>
Date: Wed 23 Sept 4:12 PM
Got ur messg. Dad. I am home but
keyless. Dumb me--left my spare up
in my room. Yeah, I know. So that
means I actually AM sitting on the
porch. Whoopsie. Total fiasco.
Sorry u were worried :>)

Thanks for calling Aimee's mom. I
am going to head over there right

now. I will call u from Aim's house
18r on ur cell. ILYL&L.

xoxo

Maddie

Madison powered down her laptop and shoved everything back into her orange bag. She pulled out the yellow windbreaker that was shoved in a side pocket, too.

Bracing herself against the drizzle, Madison headed toward the Gillespie house. Maybe this would work out better. She'd be able to finish her homework with Aimee, *and* she'd see her beloved Phin. She and Aimee could walk their dogs together after dinner the way they had always used to do when they were younger.

It wasn't raining very hard, so Madison looked up at the sky and stuck out her tongue, thirsty for a few droplets. She thought about what Gramma Helen would have said in a situation like this. She'd probably have said that this was one of those times where, "when life gives you lemons you need to make a big old pitcher of lemonade."

And what was there *really* to be glum about anyway?

Madison made a new friend that day: Madhur.

She was on her way over to her best friend Aimee's house.

And she was about to participate in a very special conference at her school.

Madison climbed up the steps to Aimee's house and knocked three times.

Doug Gillespie answered the door with a grunt and swung it open so Madison could step inside. Aimee twirled out of the shadows, dancing, as she always did.

"I am so psyched! Mom told me you were coming!" Aimee cried, lunging forward to give Madison a hug. Then Phin scooted out from around a corner and jumped right onto Madison's legs.

"Rowwoooorooooo!"

Madison grinned.

"Lemonade," she said quietly to herself. "Definitely lemonade."

## Chapter 4

School on Thursday sailed by with an uneventful sequence of classes. Poison Ivy wasn't even around in Science to make things interesting. Madison set her sights on the one potential sweet spot of the day: the first big meeting to discuss the upcoming junior leaders conference. All participating students and faculty were getting together that afternoon in the music room.

After the final bell of the school day, Madison walked down the hall toward the meeting. Mr. Gibbons had hung up large posters all along the hallway announcing the event. Madison couldn't help getting excited as she read a poster headline: JUNIOR LEADERS WANTED!

As she stopped to read the rest of the poster, Madison felt a tap on her shoulder. It was Madhur.

"On your way to the meeting?" Madhur asked.

Madison turned and smiled politely. "Yeah," she said. "What do you think a world nations luncheon is?"

"Um . . . Chinese egg rolls and french fries?" Madhur joked. "I can't imagine this cafeteria doing anything more interesting than that. Although it would be way cool if they whipped up some traditional eats, like Thai chicken, or sushi, or something a little more diverse, doncha think? My mom could come in and make aloo gobi."

"Aloo what?" Madison asked.

"Indian food," Madhur said. "My food."

Madison giggled and they walked on down the hall together. Soon they ran into Aimee and Fiona outside the music room.

"Maddie," Aimee said with her hip cocked. She held out a large tortoiseshell hair clip. "You left this on my table last night."

"Duh!" Madison pretended to smack her own forehead. "I wondered where that went. . . ."

"I am so totally jealous of you guys. Why didn't you call me, so I could come over for the sleepover, too?" Fiona said.

"The sleepover was a last-minute kind of thing," Madison said. "I was abandoned by my parents, so . . ."

"You were *abandoned*?" Madhur asked in a serious tone.

"No, no, no." Madison quickly corrected herself. "I wasn't really abandoned. I just meant that my parents weren't around—well, they were both working last night. So I went to Aimee's house for the night. She lives right up the street from me."

"Oh," Madhur said, sounding relieved, as if she'd momentarily thought that someone had really abandoned Madison. "My parents don't allow me to go to sleepovers—especially not ones during the school week."

"Bummer," Aimee said.

"Yes, they can be quite strict," Madhur said.

"So, you've never been to any sleepover . . . *ever*?" Fiona asked.

Madhur shook her head. "Never."

"Wow," Madison said. "Sleeping over at a friend's house is the best thing. You can stay up all night and gossip."

"And do makeovers," Fiona chimed in.

"Gee, I need one of those," Madhur joked. "But my parents would never approve. I once got a tube of lip gloss as a gift and Mom freaked on me. She is very traditional like that."

"My parents don't approve of half the stuff my brother and I do, either," Fiona admitted. "But that only makes it more fun, doesn't it?"

"I guess," Madhur said softly.

As the girls stood there, a rowdy group pushed past. It was all of Madison's guy friends. From the back of the group, Egg rushed over to Fiona and yelled, "Boo!" right in her face. Chet walked up with his backpack half off his shoulders and grumbled a low hello. He even said, "Wassup?" to Madhur, which was *very* strange, since Chet never said much of anything. Dan and Drew didn't speak. Their eyes were fixed on a new Gameboy that Drew held in his hand.

Hart was bringing up the rear. He came right over to Madison.

"Hey," he said sweetly.

Madison smiled self-consciously.

"Madhur," Hart added. "You guys are hanging out again, huh?"

Madison poked Hart in the shoulder. "She's in the conference, too. I told you that."

"Cool," he said. "Well, see you both inside."

He raced in to grab a seat near Egg and the other boys.

"Come on," Fiona nagged, tugging on Aimee's sweater. "We have to go get our seats now."

Madison knew Fiona wanted to get a seat near Egg. Lately, she'd been obsessed with following him everywhere—and sitting with him whenever possible. If she didn't sit close to him at lunch, she would complain about it for the rest of the day.

At the back of the music room, the conference

faculty advisers had posted various sign-up sheets and lists of names.

Madison and Madhur walked up to one of the sheets and spotted both of their names—next to each other.

"I wonder what that means?" Madison said aloud.

Madhur smiled. "It means we're partners. We're partners! That is so lucky, right?"

Madison couldn't believe it. It was luckier than lucky, indeed.

"Who's your partner, Aim?" Madison asked.

"Chet," Aimee groaned. "How could that possibly have happened? There are at least fifty other kids in this room. Why didn't I get some cute ninth-grade boy? And why isn't Ben Buckley here? Fiona, how did I get cursed with your brother?"

"Chet isn't that bad, is he?" Madhur said.

Fiona raised her eyebrows. "You obviously don't know my brother."

As it turned out, Fiona wasn't happy about her partner, either. She'd been matched up with a strange eighth-grade girl who wore baggy jeans, a T-shirt that said, "World Peace," and a dozen little pink barrettes in her hair. Of course, Fiona was trying to be upbeat about the arrangement. She always looked at the bright side.

As her friends paired off, Madison began to feel more and more grateful that she and Madhur had been matched up. It was karma.

Madison's cluster of friends sat together in the middle section of the riser seats in the music room. More and more kids filtered in and took seats around them. The room filled to capacity in no time with seventh, eighth, and ninth graders.

The faculty advisers stood in a row facing the risers: the assistant principal, Mrs. Goode; Mr. Gibbons; a couple of social-studies teachers from the upper grades; Egg's mother, Señora Diaz; and Mrs. Wing, Madison's favorite computer teacher and the school "cybrarian."

Mrs. Wing passed around a few handouts that explained in more detail the agenda for the meeting.

"I am overwhelmed by the turnout of volunteers for the conference," Mr. Gibbons said proudly. "As many of you saw at the back of the room, we have compiled a list of partners for the day of the conference and the week or so leading up to the conference. It is your job to execute the small tasks assigned to you, to do whatever research is needed, and, for some of you, to make a short presentation at the meeting itself."

Mrs. Wing reached Madison's row with the handouts. She smiled, wearing her bright red scarf and red lipstick. Madison knew she wasn't the only student who liked Mrs. Wing best, or who considered Mrs. Wing to be a role model. Lots of other kids were rushing to help this teacher out. Right now, three different boys—including Egg—jumped up to help pass out the sheets of paper Mrs. Wing carried under her arm.

On the sheet was a list of tasks that the committee was responsible for handling before and during the conference.

"Now," Mr. Gibbons began again, "let's get to work."

At some point in the middle of Mr. Gibbons's talk, Madison saw Hart, two rows ahead, turn around. Madhur must have noticed, too, because she leaned close and whispered in Madison's ear.

"He's so cute," Madhur said, grinning.

"Who?" Madison asked.

"Hart Jones, of course," Madhur said softly. "I saw you look at him, too. You guys are friends, right?"

"Yeah," Madison said. "Friends."

Madhur grinned. "I have had a crush on Hart since forever," she said.

Madison had to work hard to keep her jaw from dropping.

*Madhur had a crush on Hart?* Her *Hart*?

"Really?" Madison gulped. "You do?" Madison knew at that moment she should just tell Madhur the truth: that she and Hart were *more* than friends.

Thankfully, Fiona, Aimee, and Lindsay were not listening to their conversation. Aimee had been acting weird about Madhur since the previous day.

Even last night during their sleepover, whenever Madison mentioned Madhur, Aimee had tried to change the subject. If she found out that Madhur had a crush on Hart Jones—she would have something *big* to say about it.

Madison needed to change the subject, from Hart back to the conference—fast.

"Er . . . Madhur . . . it says here on the sheet Mrs. Wing passed out that you and I have to do research on world hunger," Madison said.

"I know," Madhur said. "I got copies of these pages yesterday when I met with Mr. Gibbons."

"You did?" Madison asked. "Wow. You really are prepared."

"My mom and dad like me to get my homework done in advance, even if it's an assignment for an after-school event like this. They're perfectionists. I like to make them happy."

Madison nodded, even though she didn't have a clue as to what Madhur was talking about. Madison's parents weren't even around half the time, due to work conflicts. They rarely checked her homework, but, rather, left that to Madison, as a part of an understood "at home" honor code. There was no prodding or dogging Madison to do more, more, and more. She was simply expected to do the best she could.

"I like to make my parents happy, too," Madison mumbled halfheartedly.

43

At that moment, Egg flicked a spitball. It hit Madison in the head. She wanted to lunge forward and throttle him. Sometimes she got tired of dealing with Egg's constant antics. She often felt like his target—and she hated it.

Mr. Gibbons shot a look in Madison and Egg's direction, as if to say, "Shhh!" But they weren't the only kids making noise. Everyone was having small side conversations, and the volume in the room was slowly building.

Mrs. Wing clapped her hands together to get their attention. Mrs. Goode played a few notes on the piano.

Everyone grew silent again.

"One of the most important parts of the conference," Mr. Gibbons finally said, "is the charitable piece. Mrs. Wing will explain this to you."

Mrs. Wing planted herself in the center of the room, waving her arms around her head as she spoke. The bracelets on her wrist jangled.

"As you know, we decided to have this small conference instead of hosting a model United Nations or a millennium conference at our school. We also decided that we would create an added feature for our meeting. We've asked the PTA to develop a special crafts and bake sale at the conference, to raise money. This money will be donated to an international cause in the name of the school and the participating students."

By the time the meeting had concluded, everyone was clear about his or her role for the weekend. The room buzzed with excitement and anticipation.

On the way out, Madhur and Madison made a plan to meet sometime that weekend to talk about their topic—and to do whatever research they needed to do. Madison figured they could work together at school or outside school. They could use the computer in either place, and the library resources would help with their conference presentation.

A few moments later, Aimee caught up with Madison at the lockers.

"Want to come over again tonight?" Aimee asked, smiling.

Madison tossed her head. "Maybe we can walk the dogs together. I don't know if Mom has another meeting tonight. When I talked to her last night, she said she might."

Aimee and Madison strolled out of school together. When they got to the glass doors in the school lobby, Hart raced past them both.

"See you later, Finnster," he called out, waving.

Madison waved back, giggling.

"Gag me," Aimee groaned.

Madison lightly punched Aimee in the side. "Quit it. At least we're not like Fiona and Egg."

"Not much," Aimee admitted. "Fiona has completely flipped—and so have you. The only sane ones left are me and Lindsay."

"Oh, right," Madison quipped.

They walked toward the curb of the parking lot in front of the school, bags swinging at their sides.

Suddenly, Aimee stopped short.

"Is that your dad?" she asked.

Madison squinted. It *was* her dad. He'd parked in the parking-lot turnaround. He waved his arms frantically in the air.

"Maddie! Over here!"

Madison and Aimee hustled over.

"What are you doing here?" Madison asked. "Is Mom in New York City again?"

Dad shook his head. "Oh, no. No, I just flew back from Boston. And the very first person I wanted to see—and surprise—was you. Want to go get ice cream with your dad?"

"Before dinner?" Madison asked.

"Dinner, schminner," Dad said. "I want a cone."

Madison giggled. "Aim, you wanna come?"

Aimee shook her head. "I can't. I have to race home and get my dance stuff. I have a rehearsal across town today, and my brother is going to drive me. Sorry, but I'd better run. Thanks a bunch for the invite, Mr. Finn."

"Abso-tootly," Dad chirped.

"Don't forget!" Aimee called out to Madison. "I have rehearsal tomorrow right after school, but we said we'd hang out around four, right?"

"Right," Madison said. "See you at your house."

"Sure thing. Bye!"

As Aimee disappeared down the street, Madison embraced Dad warmly. "It's so good to see you, Dad," she said.

"Surprises are good, right?" Dad said. "As opposed to yesterday's rainy-day disaster?"

"Oh, yeah," Madison nodded with a laugh. "Abso-tootly."

## Chapter 5

### This New Friendship

So today in the second half of lunch I was talking to Aimee in the bathroom and she started crying. Really crying. And Aimee never ever EVER cries so it was v. weird, esp. since we're @ school. I kept thinking someone like Poison Ivy would barge in and catch us there. Ivy always has perfect timing when it comes to those kinds of things.

Aim's problem is that she found out she can't do the whole future leaders' conference because it conflicts with her dance performances. She can't even TRY to do both b/c her mom said she had to choose one activity or the other. Naturally she picked dance and now she is majorly bumming b/c she thinks not doing the conference means she'll be left out of our whole grp of friends. I told her it doesn't mean that AT ALL (of course not!!!) but she won't listen. Here's the thing: Aimee hasn't said it directly but I think she's sorta jealous of this new friendship btw. Madhur & me. Is that nuts??? I've only been friends with Madhur for like a minute so what is Aim worried about? But she sounded sooo serious & sad & it bummed ME way out.

After we finished talking Aim went down to the nurse to see if she could be excused from the rest of school. I think she must have gone b/c it's almost last period anyway. What am I supposed to do to make her feel better? IS there anything I can do???

**Rude Awakening:** I used to think friendships kept sailing no matter what. So why does it feel like my ship is sinking?

I hate it when I start overthinking everything. I admit I do feel a little bit guilty about the fact that I instantly got so friendly with Madhur and invited her to the lunch table and all that, but isn't it supposed to be good to make new friends? I only wanted to share Madhur with everyone else--including Aim. The thing about Madhur

is that she comes from such a different
world and has such a different family--but
we are SO much alike.

Is it possible that 2 strangers can just
instantly connect?


"Hey," someone said, poking Madison in the shoulder.

Madison looked away from the screen and found herself face to face with none other than Hart Jones.

"Hart!" Madison cried, worried that he could read her thoughts—or even worse, her computer monitor.

But he didn't see anything. He collapsed into a chair at the side of the table where Madison was typing.

"So, what's up? What are you writing? One of your files?"

Madison felt herself get hot under the collar. She quickly hit a key that made everything onscreen disappear.

"What I am writing is none of your beeswax," Madison said, teasing him. Then she lowered her voice. "You're so nosy."

Hart leaned a little bit closer to Madison. "Why didn't you go to Mrs. Wing's today?" he whispered.

"Mrs. Wing's? For what?" Madison asked.

"Site update," Hart reminded her.

"Oh!" Madison had forgotten all about the

weekly Web site update. She was one of the school team members in charge of updating pages and downloading new photos and text to the site.

"I guess Lance can do all the work," Madison joked.

Lance was another member of their team, who was the butt of a lot of class jokes. He wasn't exactly a computer whiz—more like a computer fizz.

"But Lance isn't as sweet as you," Hart said.

Madison blushed, taken aback by his comment. Lately Hart had been saying things that caught Madison completely off guard. Although getting attention sometimes made Madison squirmy, she liked the way it made her feel deep down inside.

Hart inched closer to Madison. Was he about to grab her hands? It would be a record-breaking fourth instance of holding hands! Madison was definitely keeping count.

Just as Hart made his move, Mr. Books, the librarian, appeared.

"This is a study zone, students," Mr. Books said sternly. "Back to homework, please."

"Yes, sir," Hart said, slumping back in his chair.

As soon as Mr. Books walked away, Madison and Hart broke into silent laughter. Their faces turned watermelon red—but no noise came out.

Then someone else popped out from behind the stacks of books.

"Madison Finn," a girl said sharply.

It was Poison Ivy.

Madison jumped, startled. She swallowed her laughter.

"Hart," Ivy said, as she moved suspiciously close to him. Madison couldn't believe how Ivy continued to try to get Hart's attention—and affection—even when she knew that he was already taken.

Ivy was the queen of lost causes.

As Ivy sidled up to the chair where Hart sat, Madison counted five different times when a hand or side or some other part of Ivy touched Hart. She had made up some stupid story about needing Hart's help on a homework assignment.

*As if.* Thankfully, Madison could tell that Hart was barely listening.

After the enemy had been talking for a while, Hart turned to her and said, "I'm sorry. What did you say?"

Ivy stared back at him, dumbfounded. No words came out.

Madison wanted to burst out laughing. She bit her tongue so she wouldn't. Finally, Ivy spoke.

"By the way, I still have your notebook," Ivy growled at Madison. "I think I'll just keep it for a while. You don't mind, do you? I didn't think so. . . . Oh, well. Buh-bye."

Madison's mind raced. Ivy still had the notebook. That sneak! Madison wanted to scream out after the enemy, but she couldn't lose her cool here. She didn't want Mr. Books to come back over to reprimand her.

"Just ignore her," Hart whispered. "Ivy's so lame. She's always hanging around and trying to talk to me these days, but *ugh*. I used to think she was nicer, but . . . well . . ."

"But what?" Madison couldn't help asking.

"But *you're* the nice one," Hart said plainly. "You know that."

Madison stood up. "I really should go," she said, extending her hand. It just hovered out there, waiting for someone to grab it.

Would Hart take it and hold it in his own? Madison hoped so. She was going for a fifth handholding right there; right then.

Hart stood up.

Madison held her breath.

Then, in one slo-mo moment, Hart grabbed Madison's hand. He squeezed it so all the fingers pinched together.

"Want me to carry your book bag?" Hart asked.

Madison readjusted the orange messenger bag on her shoulder while still managing *not* to let go of Hart's hand.

"I'm okay," she said coyly, savoring the moment. "I've got it." She wished she could add, "And I've got you, too, and *how cool is that*?"

Of course, the library was no place for slick

movie-of-the-week lines. She'd save the line for her files, where no thought was too cheesy or too forward.

The two of them kept holding hands all the way down the stairs to the first floor. By the time they reached the front door of the school, and Madison and Hart had to let go, they both had sweaty palms. Now it was time for the day's good-byes. Hart had basketball practice, and Madison needed to head over to the animal clinic. It was after three o'clock; Dan was meeting her at the bus stop.

"E me later," Madison suggested to Hart as they parted ways.

"Sure," he said, although Madison was pretty sure he wouldn't. Guys weren't always so good about calling or e-mailing, even if they promised. They certainly weren't as good as BFFs.

As Hart walked away, Madhur appeared.

"Hey! I was just thinking about you!" Madison said, stretching the truth a little. "We have to talk more about what we're doing for the conference."

"I know," Madhur nodded. "I told my mother about our being partners. She said I should invite you over this weekend for supper. We could do work in the afternoon and then you could stay to eat. Everyone in my house cooks on Sundays."

"Wow," Madison said, grinning. "That sounds fun. I would . . . well, I have to ask my mom or dad first, actually. Can I E you later?"

"I don't have e-mail, remember?" Madhur said.

"Oh, of course," Madison said. "Um . . . can I just call you at home?"

Madhur nodded. "That's what I was going to do—if I didn't see you here at school this afternoon. But I saw you, so . . ."

"Where are you headed right now?" Madison asked.

"To the library," Madhur said softly. "I have a lot of homework."

"You do?" Madison asked. "I didn't think the teachers were giving that much reading this week. . . ."

"No. I'm a few chapters ahead of the rest of the class."

"Oh, I forgot. You do all your homework way in advance," Madison said.

"Where are you going?" Madhur asked.

"I'm on my way to the Far Hills Animal Clinic. My friend Dan and I are volunteers there. These kittens got sick and died, and . . . well, it's a sad story. I told Dan I would help him out this afternoon."

"The animal clinic? Wow," Madhur said.

"I remember from your speech in class that you like animals a lot, right?"

Madhur nodded. "For sure."

"Do you want to come to the clinic with us?" Madison asked.

"Oh, no." Madhur demurred. "I couldn't. I mean,

my parents don't know about it, and I shouldn't. I don't take the bus alone. . . ."

"You won't be alone," Madison said. "We'll be with you. And it's only two stops away."

Madhur looked conflicted. "I can't. Really."

Madison didn't want to press the issue. But then she said, "I could introduce you to all the animals. You'd love it."

A wide smile spread across Madhur's face. "Okay. I guess my parents won't mind. I'll go."

Just then, Dan appeared, and the trio raced to catch one of the local buses that passed the clinic. Dan told Madison he was happy to see an extra volunteer.

Dan's mom, who worked the front desk at the clinic, was overjoyed to see three helpers coming to the clinic that afternoon—even if Madison and Madhur would only be there for a short time. Madison took Madhur into the back and showed her the rows of animal cages where dogs in all shapes and sizes barked their hellos.

"This place is great," Madhur said, leaning toward a cage with a little dog inside.

Dan opened the cage and pulled out the dog, a small Pomeranian. He cradled the dog in his arms and then passed it over to Madhur.

"Wanna hold her?" Dan said. "Her name is Polly Doodle. Don't ask."

Madhur laughed as she took Polly from him. "Oh, you are so cute! Just the cutest thing ever, ever, ever."

Madison giggled. "That's what *I* always say," she joked.

"I know it's a huge bummer, but we have to deal with the kittens, Maddie," Dan interrupted.

He explained to Madison and Madhur that the animals had already been cremated; they just needed to be buried, out behind the clinic, where there was a garden with little pet headstones for animals who died during a stay at the clinic or the shelter.

"This is weird," Madhur said as they stepped into the little pet cemetery. "But sweet."

"Sweet?" Dan said. "Man, sugar is sweet. This just stinks."

"Dan doesn't like saying good-bye," Madison said. "We get pretty attached to the animals here. You know?"

Madhur nodded. "I know. I lost a pet once. It's hard."

Dan said a few words over a large sign he'd made with the names of all the kittens written on it. Then Madison said a few more words, and Madhur said her own good-bye.

"Oh, man," Dan groaned when they'd finished up. "It's after four o'clock. I have to help my mom with these parrots that are coming in tonight. This guy has three birds, and they're all getting surgery."

Madison made a face. "What kind of surgery?"

Dan just shook his head. "Don't ask." He said that a lot.

"I'd better get home," Madhur said. "I told my mom I'd be home by four thirty. If she finds out I came here *and* I'm late . . ."

All at once, Madison's face grew pale. *It was after four o'clock?*

"Oh!" she blurted out, scrambling back inside to pick up her orange bag.

"What's the matter?" Dan asked, following her.

Madhur chased after the two of them.

"It's after four," Madison said, "and I promised Aimee I would—" she sighed. "I promised," she groaned.

"It's not that much later. She'll understand," Madhur said sweetly. "That's what friends do. They understand you. Right?"

"Normally. Except that Aimee had this terrible day today, and I just . . . I better go. . . ."

"Call me back about Sunday, okay?" Madhur asked.

Madison stopped short. "We should see each other before that. Why don't you come out tomorrow night with us?"

"Is it family night?" Madhur asked.

"Not exactly. Depends on what you mean by 'family.' My parents are divorced," Madison said.

"Oh," Madhur said.

"Don't worry. I'm used to the Big D—that's what I call their 'divorce.' Besides, Dad is married again now. And I like my stepmom a lot. I think my mom will probably get married again sometime, too. Then again, she's married to her job. . . ."

"Don't you have to go?" Dan asked.

"Oh . . . yeah . . ." Madison said. She felt a little flustered. Aimee was waiting. But she wanted to make a plan with Madhur, too. For some reason, she couldn't shut up.

"You see, I usually have dinner with Dad on random Saturdays, but tomorrow, for some reason, he declared it GNO, or Girls' Night Out—except for him, of course. I'm bringing Aimee, Fiona, and Lindsay to dinner with us. We might go bowling or catch a movie, too. And the reason I'm telling you all this is because . . . well . . . you should come."

"Me?" Madhur asked.

"Why not?" Madison answered.

"It sounds like fun. Of course, it is short notice. I would have to ask my parents," Madhur said. "Sometimes they plan my weekends for me."

"They have to let you come! Then we can study *and* have a lot of fun this weekend," Madison said, her pulse racing. She was already running late—and Aimee was *still* waiting. She had to hurry.

At the front of the clinic, Madison and Madhur swept past a woman carrying a large yellow tabby with oversize ears.

"That's one fat cat," Dan whispered. Then he turned and said, "See you later."

"So long," the girls said in unison. Near the

front door, they eyed a trio of parrots in cages.

"So long to you, too," they sqawked in unison at the birds. "Good luck in surgery."

Leaving the squat clinic building, Madhur made a sharp left, toward her own neighborhood, just a short walk away. "I'll let you know about tomorrow," she said as she walked away.

Madison heard but didn't say anything. She was too busy making her own sharp right, walking fast, fast, FAST toward the bus. With a lot of luck, she might just make it home to Aimee and the dogs by four thirty—or at least by five.

She hoped Aimee wouldn't be too disappointed.

# Chapter 6

<MadFinn>: Im sooo glad ur online
  now
<Bigwheels>: I got yr email this AM
  wassup???
<MadFinn>: Aim's MAM
<Bigwheels>: Y?
<MadFinn>: I sorta blew her off
  yesterday by mistake
<Bigwheels>: :{o}
<MadFinn>: I 4got we were supposed
  2 meet and then she was waiting 4
  me and now it's REALLY bad b/c
  we're all going 2 dinner 2nite
<Bigwheels>: just u & aim r going?
<MadFinn>: no, it's the whole group.

It's us & Fiona & Lins & Madhur 2
<Bigwheels>: Madhur???
<MadFinn>: OMG I can't believe I
   didn't tell u she is the coolest
   new friend @ school she's always
   been here but we never knew each
   other until this whole leader's
   confrnec thing
<MadFinn>: conference (sorry)
<Bigwheels>: wow she sounds nice but
   the sitch sounds icky
<MadFinn>: that's the understatement
   of the yr :>P
<Bigwheels>: WAYG2D?
<MadFinn>: be super nice to Aimee
   all nite I guess
<Bigwheels>: good plan
<MadFinn>: how's life in Washington?
<Bigwheels>: My bro is doing good
   and we are getting a dog--can u
   believe it?
<MadFinn>: Yeah, it seems like ur
   always getting a new pet
<Bigwheels>: How's Phinnie??
<MadFinn>: Fat LOL he's eating 2
   many dog treats he found the bin
   in the kitchen closet and ate an
   entire box the other day
<Bigwheels>: <LMFO>
<MadFinn>: OMG it's late I better
   get going

```
<Bigwheels>: GL 2nite
<MadFinn>: (((TAL)))
<Bigwheels>: smooch
```

Madison logged off and double-checked the clock. On the outside, Madison was dressed and ready to go. But on the inside it was a different story. She wasn't ready at all. Girls' Night Out with Dad and the BFFs had started out as a simple, fun idea. But now, thanks to Madison's impromptu invitation to Madhur and Aimee's sulking, things had grown more complicated.

As soon as Madhur's mom spoke to Madison's mom, parental permission had been granted for both the Saturday and the Sunday night events. Madhur would join the BFF crew, and Madison would join the Singhs, for a traditional Indian dinner. It was all good. Or was it?

There was Aimee to consider.

After being made to wait for more than an hour alone while Madison raced home from the clinic, Aimee had had her feelings hurt once already that weekend. She felt so let down that she'd threatened to bail on GNO—despite Madison's zillion apologies. Fiona got involved, too, calling Aimee on the telephone and begging her to come no matter what.

Just like that, a low-key event turned into major drama.

Madison was feeling the pressure.

She paced across her bedroom carpet, the soles of her boots rubbing the carpet one way and then another. She thought of all the things she should say to get back into Aimee's good graces. There was no worse feeling than having a BFF madder than mad at her. Aimee was good at holding grudges, too.

Deep down, Madison wondered if Madhur's presence at GNO might present even *more* problems.

"Honey bear!" Mom called from downstairs. "It's nearly five o'clock, and Dad will be here soon. Where are your friends?"

Madison scanned the front lawn from her bedroom window. She didn't see anyone coming up the driveway or walking on either side of the sidewalk.

Had Aimee decided to go ahead and boycott anyway?

Then the doorbell rang.

"Rowowooorroooo!" Phin howled. Madison heard his little nails go clickety-click across the wooden floors downstairs. She listened closely as Mom answered the front door.

"Hello," a soft voice said from below. "I am Madison's new friend, Madhur Singh. I think she's expecting me. . . ."

"Madhur! Yes!" Mom cried. "How are you?"

Madison checked her reflection in the bedroom mirror and raced to the top of the stairs.

"You're here!" Madison said as she took the steps two at a time on her way down to greet Madhur.

Madhur smiled. "My dad is always early, and he drove me, so . . ."

"Why don't you two wait in the living room until the other girls arrive?" Mom suggested.

Madison and Madhur went in and sat down on opposite sides of the room.

"Nice outfit," Madison said, checking out Madhur's clothes. Over a long-sleeved yellow T-shirt, Madhur wore a violet-colored sweater and dark jeans that looked as if they had been ironed. Around her shoulders, Madhur had wrapped a long, colorful scarf with dime-size round mirrors woven into the pattern. In some ways, nothing seemed to match; yet it all worked together perfectly. "I really like your scarf, too," Madison said.

"My grandmamma made it for me," Madhur said. "She's a good seamstress."

"That's funny," Madison grinned. "My grandma always knits me a new scarf every year. Usually for winter."

"That *is* funny," Madhur said. "Our grand-mothers are alike. Cool."

Phin trotted over to where Madhur was sitting. He sniffed at her red loafers, and she shifted in the chair.

"Hello, doggy," Madhur said.

"Phinnie," Madison interjected. "That's his name, Phineas T. Finn."

"Like Phineas T. Barnum the circus guy?" Madhur asked.

Madison grinned. Madhur was the only person who'd ever correctly guessed the origin of Phin's name.

"Cool," Madhur said again. It seemed to be her favorite word. "I love the circus."

A clock on a table in the hall clanged even though it wasn't five o'clock yet.

"That clock's fast . . ." Madison said. "But my dad should be here soon. . . . I hope . . ." She eyed the door.

*Drrrrring.*

Both girls jumped—and laughed at that coincidence, too. Madison raced to answer it.

But it wasn't Dad—yet.

"Fiona!" Madison cried. "Come inside. We're still waiting for Lindsay and Aimee."

"I just saw Lindsay down the driveway. She was in her dad's fire truck," Fiona said with a chuckle.

"Lindsay's father is a fireman?" Madhur asked.

Madison and Fiona cracked up. "No!" they said in unison.

"He just drives this cool red sports car. For some wacky reason, Lindsay calls it the fire truck," Madison said.

"Oh," Madhur said meekly. She looked embarrassed at having misunderstood.

When Fiona entered the house, she left the front door open; and Lindsay came right inside a moment later.

"Hello? Anybody home? Hello? I know you're here. . . ." Lindsay called out.

Madison raced into the entryway and threw her arms around Lindsay. "Ready for Girls' Night Out?" she cried excitedly.

Lindsay rolled her eyes. "Duh," she said. "What do *you* think? Do you think we might see Dan or some of the other guys tonight?"

"Dan, Dan, Dan . . ." Fiona chuckled. "He's all you think about lately."

"Not true!" Lindsay cried. Then she noticed Madhur standing there. "Oh, hey, Madhur. Are you coming tonight, too?"

"The more the merrier, right?" Fiona added cheerily.

Just then, Dad appeared at the threshold with his arms crossed, his car keys dangling precariously from his fingers. He stepped to the side dramatically to reveal Aimee behind him. She waved but didn't speak right away.

"So, is the whole crew here?" Dad asked.

Madison waited for Aimee to make some crack the way she always did, but Aimee said nothing. She lingered on the porch, lips buttoned as tightly as her denim jacket.

Madison gave Dad an enormous squeeze hello just as Mom came back out to say good-bye. Then everyone headed out to the car. Everything about the scene felt a little forced. Madison secretly hoped that within ten minutes everyone would be buckled into their seats in Dad's car, gossiping and laughing. How could she help to break the tension?

"Wow, Mr. Finn," Fiona cried as they raced down the driveway. "New wheels?"

Dad smirked. He and Stephanie, Madison's stepmother, had just purchased a new SUV that could seat seven people. Dad proudly opened the door, and everyone shuffled in, vying for the cushiest seats.

Lindsay crawled into the back. Aimee followed behind. Fiona sat in the middle with Madhur next to her. Madison rode shotgun, as usual, with Dad at the wheel.

It was torture being up front with her dad rather than in the back with her friends, but Madison accepted the seating arrangements. They'd be at the mall in no time anyway.

Dad talked nonstop. He had the entire evening planned out.

"First, we'll head over to Cracker Wheel, the new diner at the mall. It's a real scene," he explained. "We may have to wait for a table, but there's plenty to do around the mall."

"There's a new accessory place—" Fiona started to say.

"Boogie's!" Lindsay interrupted. "It's so amazing. I went there last week with my Aunt Mimi."

"Can we stop in at the dance shop?" Aimee asked.

"Are you a dancer?" Madhur asked.

Madison turned around in time to catch Aimee's hard stare. "Um, yeah . . ." Aimee said. "It's what I do."

"She's one of the stars at Madame Elaine's ballet school in town," Madison piped up from the front seat.

"I love dance," Madhur said. "My mother was a *Banghra* dancer in India."

Aimee's face seemed to brighten a little bit. "What's that?"

"It's a Punjabi folk dance," Madhur said. "My mom was the best. I can't dance it—or anything else—to save my life," she added, with a laugh and a toss of her head.

Madison and Lindsay laughed, too. "Neither can we!" they said at the same time.

Dad pulled in to the lower-level parking garage at the Far Hills Shoppes. The GNO group exited the car and paraded through the main doors, into the atrium of the mall, jaws flapping and eyes scanning the crowds for familiar faces—and good stores.

"Our dinner reservation is for five forty-five," Dad said, checking his watch. "We have a few minutes to spare. You girls want to shop around a bit?"

"Do you even have to ask?" Madison said with a wide grin. She spotted a new kiosk a few yards away. "There's always something to check out. We'll meet you at the restaurant in fifteen minutes, okay?"

Dad gave the girls a casual salute and went on his way.

"Look at all of those hats!" Fiona cried, running over to the kiosk. She immediately picked up a captain's hat with a giant blue feather in the brim and placed it on her head. "Ahoy, mateys," she said, in her best pirate snarl.

Madison and Madhur couldn't help laughing.

Aimee grabbed a hat next. It was a pink tiara (of course), with rhinestones in a heart shape on top.

"Your Majesty," Fiona said.

Meanwhile, Lindsay found an oversize red-and-white-striped Dr. Seuss hat that flopped in her face.

"Try one on, Maddie," Fiona begged, handing Madison a Sherlock Holmes–type hat. "This one is so you."

"Well . . ." Madison hesitated before putting it on her head. "Elementary, my dear Fiona."

"Madison, do you want to be a detective?" Madhur asked.

"She wishes!" Aimee said.

Madhur topped her own head with a large-brimmed sombrero and began to dance around. "Olé!" she sang. "This is so much fun. Thanks for letting me join you tonight."

Madison smiled. Fiona and Lindsay nodded. Aimee just said, "Whatever."

A short, squat man in a woolly sweater came

around from behind the kiosk. His eyes got very wide as he spoke.

"Ladies! Ladies! Read the sign, ladies!" the man barked.

Madison looked up and saw the sign he was talking about, with its bold, black letters.

NO TOUCHING OR TRYING ON THE HATS!
YOU TRY—YOU BUY! THIS IS NOT A COSTUME CART!

"Whoopsie," Aimee said when she read the sign. She quickly removed her tiara.

"You try, you buy?" Lindsay repeated, staring at the man. "But we're just having—"

"Put the hats back," the man commanded.

"But hats are meant to be tried on," Madhur said softly.

The man shot her a look. "Not my hats," he said.

"Wow, I guess we won't be able to buy those ten hats we wanted for the party, then," Madhur said swiftly, turning back toward the other girls. "We should go away like he says. We'll have to buy at that *other* kiosk."

"Ten hats? Party?" The man was caught off guard. "What other kiosk?"

Madison was about to explode with laughter, and she knew the other girls were ready to burst, too. As Madhur led them away from the kiosk, the BFFs tried their best to keep all their giggles inside.

The man spluttered, trying to get them to turn back.

"Wait!" the man cried. "Come back."

But the girls were long gone, on their way to meet Madison's dad.

"That was a good trick," Fiona said when they were out of earshot of the kiosk. "I hate to say it, but . . ."

"You rock!" Madison cried, smiling. She hurried to catch up with Madhur and the others.

"Very impressive," Lindsay said.

Madison stood back a bit, waiting to see how Aimee would respond. Had the tension in the group broken? It felt that way, at least for now. The cluster of BFFs had grown larger by one person for GNO, and everything was shaping up to be just fine.

Dinner flew by. Dad didn't have to do much talking, because the girls monopolized the conversation, between bites of fried chicken and salad. Madison sensed that Dad was probably a little overwhelmed. He shot her little stares all through dinner, raising his eyebrows and rolling his eyes as if he were speaking in some kind of secret code.

Rather than get dessert at the restaurant, Dad suggested they skip over to the multiplex for a movie and chocolate candy.

The girls didn't need much convincing. Within moments, the group headed over to the movie theater and stood behind the crowd that had begun to gather outside the ticket window and doors.

Madison ducked away with Dad to get into the ticket line.

When she and Dad rejoined the group after five minutes, tickets in hand, it was no longer just a group of girlfriends.

Egg, Dan, Drew, Chet, *and* Hart had shown up.

Was this another weird coincidence? Madison thought.

"Isn't this great?" Fiona said as she sidled up to Egg. There was no doubt about her feelings on the situation.

"Wait. What are you guys doing here. This is supposed to be GNO," Madison said firmly.

"Are you boys here with a chaperone?" Dad inquired, looking around.

"My mom's here . . . somewhere . . ." Egg said nonchalantly. "But she left us to watch the movie while she shops or whatever."

"I see, I see," Dad said. "And she doesn't know that you were planning to meet the girls here, does she?"

"Well," Egg stammered. "N—n—not exactly."

Dad nodded. "I see again. Well, I'm here. I should be chaperone enough."

"Dad, please," Madison implored. "You're embarrassing me in front of my friends."

Dad shrugged. "Maddie, it's official. Your GNO just turned into SGNO."

"What's SGNO?" Madison asked, looking mortified.

"Seventh grader night out," Dad said, smiling. "Come on. Let's go, everyone."

As they walked inside the theater, Madison noticed Madhur off to the side. Chet was standing with her, talking. They both wore wide grins. What was going on?

Everyone selected their snack of choice and headed in to the dimly lit theater. The choice of seating was critical.

*Who would sit where?*

Fiona and Egg paired off, naturally. No surprises there. Then Lindsay and Dan sat together. They had only just begun to open up about their feelings of "like" for each other. Then, just as Chet was about to slide into the row, he bumped into Madhur, and the two of them ended up sitting together. Madison parked herself on the other side. Hart grabbed the seat near Madison, followed by Aimee (who still wasn't saying much), and then Drew. Boy-girl-boy-girl always worked out best. Dad hung back at the end, looking a little concerned. Madison knew why. He was probably thinking about what everyone would do in the darkness of a movie theater. Luckily, he kept his lip zipped.

Madhur and Chet giggled through the first five minutes of previews. Madison couldn't help hearing—and staring at—them. Hart was trying to get Madison's attention, but she wasn't listening. When Chet finally turned in the other direction, Madison seized the moment.

"What's up with *him*?" Madison asked Madhur under her breath.

"Who?" Madhur asked sweetly.

"Chet," Madison whispered.

Madhur shrugged. "Everything. Nothing. I don't know."

"Yes, you do," Madison insisted.

"What are you talking about?" Chet asked.

Madison sank backward in her chair again, embarrassed.

"Nothing," she said.

As the words *Feature Presentation* appeared onscreen, questions darted in and out of Madison's mind. What had happened to Madison's well-laid plans for GNO? Why was Aimee still giving her the silent treatment? Why did *everything* have to end up a complete mess?

Then—without warning—Hart grabbed Madison's hand. That made six times. It took her breath away.

And as she stared down at his fingers and the movie started, all the buzzing inside Madison's head just . . . stopped.

# Chapter 7

Madison opened up her laptop and logged on to bigfishbowl.com. The date flashed up in the corner: HAPPY SUNDAY!

"So you come to this main screen," Madison explained to Madhur, "and from here we have to assign you a password and all that."

Madison had decided that she would make it a top priority to get Madhur online, with her own bigfishbowl e-mail address. They sat together at Madhur's house, on a long, ornate living-room sofa covered with quilts and coverlets decorated with fringes and the same little mirrors Madison had seen on Madhur's scarf. Once Mom had given the thumbs-up to Madison's having dinner at the Singh house,

Madison knew it would be an ideal time to bring her trusty orange messenger bag and laptop with its wireless chip.

"What password do you want?" Madison asked.

"I don't know," Madhur said, thinking very hard.

"My latest password is 'Files'," Madison said in a low voice, as if she were trading undercover information. "I change it once a month, for security purposes—not that anyone would really ever try to break into my files or my mailbox . . ."

"I guess I could make 'Punjab' my password, for starters," Madhur said.

"That's good," Madison said.

Within moments of having registered, an e-mail appeared in Madhur's new e-mailbox. It stated that she was officially registered on the "funniest fishtank online."

```
From: No_Reply@bigfishbowl.com
To: MadSingh
Subject: CONFIRMATION
Date: Sun 27 Sept 4:09 PM
This is a confirmation e-mail.
Do not reply. If you have any
questions, contact the Webmaster.

New bigfishbowl member: MADHUR
Age: 12 (permission granted)
Screen name: MADSINGH
Password: Punjab
```

Please keep this e-mail in a safe place in case you should lose your account information.

Thanks for swimming in the fishbowl!

Sincerely,

Shark and the Administrative Team

Madhur had now officially acquired her own screen name, password, and access to the world of bigfishbowl. Madison instantly felt more connected than ever to her new friend.

Glancing around, Madison noticed the way the living room was crammed full of large pieces of furniture, all draped in blankets. Atop the fireplace mantel sat two painted figurines. One had the head of an elephant; its front legs were raised. It was dressed in flowing clothes. The other looked more human, only with blue skin. Madhur explained that the elephant figure was called Sri Ganesha. "My mom and grandmamma always talk to Ganesha before anything important happens. Sometimes I even do it, too, like before a big test," Madhur said.

"Does it work?" Madison asked.

"Well, Ganesha is the lord of wisdom, I guess, so he knows a lot. And he has all the energy of Shiva. That's the other figure, by the way, the blue guy.

78

He is the destroyer of evil and the restorer of good."

"Why is he blue?" Madison asked.

"Because he drank poison to save the world from destruction," Madhur stated matter-of-factly. "And he turned blue."

"Oh," Madison said. "That's intense."

"Yeah," Madhur said. "With a capital I."

Along one long shelf attached to a wall, Madison spotted rows of framed photographs. Some were pictures of more statues of Ganesha and Shiva—but most were real-people pictures of Madhur and the members of her family. There were old-fashioned, sepia-toned photos alongside Polaroid shots that had been placed in teeny frames.

"What's that smell?" Madison asked, sniffing at the air. All at once a pungent, sweet aroma filled the living room.

Madhur shrugged her shoulders. "My mother is preparing a tandoori dinner tonight," she said. "She's making lamb and chicken. I hope you like meat. Once I had a friend come over and she was a vegetarian. I thought she'd keel over when my mom served her a kebab on rice."

Madison giggled. "My mom's a vegetarian; I'm not."

"Do you like bread? My mother makes the best *kulchas*. Those are stuffed Indian breads. We have all these dipping sauces for them, too."

Madison swore she felt her stomach flip-flop—with hunger.

"Okay, girls, I need your help," Mrs. Singh said, sashaying into the living room in her traditional garb "Maddie, I need you in the kitchen now." Madison was surprised to hear Mrs. Singh use her nickname. Then she realized Mrs. Singh was speaking to Madhur.

"Your mom calls you Maddie?" Madison asked Madhur. For some reason, Madison had not even considered the possibility that she and Madhur would share not only the same interests—but also the exact same nickname, Maddie.

"For as long as I can remember," Madhur said.

"Maddie is *my* nickname, too, you know," Madison said.

"So, which of us will be Maddie One and which will be Maddie Two?" Madhur joked.

Mrs. Singh showed the girls into the very large kitchen. Stretched across one counter was an array of ingredients Madison had never seen. Then again, Mom rarely cooked, so these items wouldn't have been familiar. There were jars of cardamom, curry, aniseed, saffron, and tamarind. Although she had no idea what any of those tasted like, Madison's mouth watered at the thought of them. The room smelled like a spice chest.

"Don't forget ghee," Mrs. Singh explained to the girls.

"That's butter," Madhur whispered.

Madison nodded and watched. The meal magically came together.

Somewhere between Mrs. Singh's rubbing the spices onto the chicken and Madhur's stuffing the Indian bread with herbs and onions, an older boy plowed through the kitchen doors. He carried an iPod and wore a hat pulled down over his forehead.

"Yo!" the boy said.

"Who's that?" Madison whispered, curious.

"Mister Obnoxious," Madhur mumbled, "Otherwise known as my brother. He is seriously lacking the cool gene."

"You have a brother?" Madison said quietly. For some reason, she'd assumed Madhur was an only child—just as she was. After all, they'd been alike in so many other ways.

"Are you staying for supper, Jahan?" Mrs. Singh asked, reaching over to remove the boy's headphones. She turned back to Madison. "Jahan is just back from year two at university. He's studying to be a doctor."

"We're so lucky to be graced by his presence," Madhur said mockingly, making a face at him.

"Zip it," Jahan said as he shot a brooding look toward Madison and Madhur. "Sorry, Mom, I can't stay for supper."

Mrs. Singh hit Jahan in the shoulder with a wooden spoon. "Nonsense," she said, chastising him. "Of course you will stay. Now, go put out the silver and china—for five today."

Jahan skulked away. Madison and Madhur couldn't help giggling.

"So where's Dad?" Jahan asked, ignoring Madison's and his sister's laughter.

Mrs. Singh smiled. "Your father is upstairs. You know. Napping."

"Snoring is more like it," Jahan said.

"He'll be down for the meal," Madhur's mom said.

Everyone laughed at Jahan's comment, including Madison, even though she knew it was a family joke. Everything about Madhur's family was different from Madison's own; yet it was so *comfortable*.

Somewhere inside, a twinge of jealousy bubbled up. Madison tried to ignore it. What was making her jealous? Then she knew. It was Madhur's intact family: mom, dad, *and* brother.

Madison often felt a similar jealous twinge when she visited Aimee or Fiona. It was always the same realization: having two parents at home was somehow better than having one. Okay, not always better, but *different*, in a way that made Madison miss life *before* the Big D. No matter how much she got used to her parents' divorce, she'd always long for a mom and a dad who lived in the same house. And having a stepmother (Stephanie) didn't really help. An extra person couldn't just make all those other feelings go away.

Madison recalled how, pre–Big D, Dad had

82

prepared delicious meals in their house, just as as Mrs. Singh was doing now, in hers. Phin had used to dance around the table while Mom filled water glasses. Life hadn't just been a series of paper plates and takeout. Sometimes, these days, that was how life felt.

"Maddie?" Madhur asked. "It feels funny to say my own nickname when I talk to you."

Madison smiled politely and tried to get her thoughts back on track.

"Let's go hang out upstairs for a few minutes," Madhur said. "Supper won't be ready for a little while."

Madison followed her new friend up a long, winding staircase. At the top, the hall split three ways. Madhur went through an orange door. This had to be a very good sign: Madhur's door was painted orange! That was Madison's favorite color in the whole world.

"Welcome to my room!" Madhur announced.

The room was tiny, Madison observed, but bright, like a bouquet of flowers. The walls were painted in rich red, yellow, and tangerine, respectively. On her bed, Madhur had a collection of colorful stuffed fish. The room looked like a rainbow come to life.

"You like fish," Madison asked, "and you had never been on bigfishbowl!" That had to be more than just a coincidence.

Madhur smiled. "Maybe," she said.

It was almost too crowded with two girls in the small room at once, but Madison loved being there. Her mood improved instantly as they lay across Madhur's bed, legs waving in the air. Then Madhur pulled out a thick photo album.

"This is a photo of my grandmamma when she was little," Madhur explained, showing Madison a small picture of a young girl, half dressed, smiling, standing next to a wide river. Next to the girl, a cluster of Punjabi women kneeled by the water washing clothes.

"She looks so small, standing there," Madison commented. The sepia-toned photo had been taken in Punjab more than seventy years before.

Madhur flipped through the pages. There was an incredible array of photos of India and Pakistan and of many generations of Singhs, taken over the years. Madison thought about her own photo albums at home. She didn't have photos of exotic places—not like this. There were some pictures that had been taken on Mom's film shoots, but nothing seemed as impressive or as exciting as Madhur's family album.

Madison dreaded the thought, but it popped into her head nonetheless: was her life *boring*?

Of course, Madison was grateful for everything she had, and of course she had lots of people in her world who loved her, and of course she did *some* interesting things. Mom's job had afforded Madison the opportunity of traveling some. But she didn't have all these cousins or grandmothers or uncles or even pets. She didn't have stories like the ones Madhur's grandmamma told.

Madison tried to keep up as Madhur continued with her running commentary on the places and people in the photos. After a half hour, the subject finally switched to homework. The girls remained stuck on what topic to choose for the project. There were many issues, affecting the whole world. What would theirs be?

"MADDIE!"

A booming voice roared upstairs.

"Who was that?" Madison asked.

"My brother," Madhur grumbled. "He's such a loudmouth. I guess it's suppertime. We should go."

Madhur hopped off the bed; Madison followed. They went downstairs and back into the kitchen, where many different-size plates and bowls and steaming hot cups of rice were spread across a pat-terned table runner. There was that pungent, warm, spicy smell again.

*Mmmmmmmm.*

Mr. Singh appeared, still a little groggy from his nap. He had a beard and mustache, although he did not have much hair on the top of his head.

"Aha!" Mr. Singh announced, taking a seat at the head of the table. He smiled broadly at Madison. "At last! Our guest of honor has arrived."

Madhur nudged Madison and leaned in to

whisper, "Don't worry. My dad likes to make a big deal. He won't bite."

Madison took her seat at the table next to Madhur. Jahan sat directly across the table from them both, but he didn't say much. He seemed to be wearing imaginary headphones, trying hard to tune out everyone else. Mrs. Singh sat at the opposite end of the table from her husband and began to serve food onto a plate.

"So, Madhur tells me your name is Maddie, too. Does that make you sweet lightning, too?" Mr. Singh laughed.

Madison looked bewildered, but Madhur cleared things up immediately.

"Dad's talking about my first and middle names, which are Madhur Damini. That literally means 'sweet lightning.' Dad always says I have this special spark. Cheesy, right?"

"Not at all. My middle name is just Francesca. I have no idea what it means, or what 'Madison' means, for that matter."

"You should look it up on bigfishbowl!" Madhur said brightly.

Everyone dug in to the dishes. Madison spooned little tastes of the tandoori chicken, lentil daal, palak paneer, biryani, lamb kebab, and more out onto her plate. She'd eaten Indian food before, of course, but nothing that compared to this meal. Everything tasted delicious. Or maybe the company made it so.

At some point during dinner, the family conversation turned to school. Madhur reported on how she had done on the last paper for English, as well as her results on a pop quiz in social studies class. Madison never had to report in to her mom like that. She wondered if Mr. and Mrs. Singh would ask about Madison's grades, too. But thankfully, Madhur was doing all the talking.

Mr. Singh listened intently as the subject switched to that of the school conference. His face broke into a crooked grin again as Madhur mentioned the presentation with Madison.

"So, Dad, we decided to do our presentation on world hunger," Madhur said.

"Makes sense," Jahan interjected. "Since you eat so much."

"If I wanted your opinion . . ." Madhur started to say, but Mr. Singh held up his hand to cut her off.

"Tell me more about the project," he said, pressing for particulars.

Madison kept quiet while Madhur explained. Madhur talked about poverty and signing petitions and saving the world. She sounded really knowledgeable.

"Good, good," Mr. Singh said. "You see how even one small presentation in school can make a difference. You must look at every academic opportunity as a moment when you stand and let your voice be heard."

*"ACK!"*

Jahan broke up the conversation when he nearly choked on some kind of bone. He gulped a glass of water as Madhur cracked up.

"Choke much?" Madhur said. "That's one way to be heard, all right."

"Very funny," Jahan cracked back. "Mom, this tandoori is a little hot, no?"

"No. You like it hot," Mrs. Singh said. "Hush."

Jahan settled back into his seat, stewing. The rest of the meal passed by more quietly as they talked about other subjects besides the conference. Mr. and Mrs. Singh engaged in a brief but humorous debate about their neighbor's pet cats.

"Sorry about my parents," Madhur said to Madison near the end of the meal, rolling her eyes. "Utter mortification."

"Not at all," Madison said, shaking her head. "Parent stuff. I get it. Except what was all that stuff about world hunger? We hadn't officially decided on a topic, had we?"

"Oh," Madhur said quickly. "I was just thinking on my feet. There was no way I could avoid telling my dad about the project. If I said we were undecided, he would have given us a very hard time."

Madison appreciated the fact that there was a lot of pressure in Madhur's home to do things the "right" way.

"Sure," Madison said. "Besides, it's a great idea.

And we can pull the whole thing together this week, right?"

"I hope so," Madhur said. "We've been spending more time being friends than doing what we're supposed to do, you know?"

"I guess so," Madison said.

"We were assigned to each other to do the work, not to hang out at the movies," Madhur went on.

"Right," Madison said. Inside she was thinking, Is hanging at the movies so bad?

Madhur must have been thinking the same thing, because a moment later she added, "Not that I don't like the movies. And, your friends are all so nice. . . ."

"Especially Chet, right? I saw you talking to him a lot," Madison said.

"Yeah. Hart, too," Madhur added. "He really is cute, isn't he?"

"Who?" Madison stammered.

"Hart, of course. Everyone thinks so."

"They do?" *This was the time to say something*, Madison thought. *Say something.*

"I have a little crush," Madhur admitted. "Is that wrong?"

*Yes! Yes! Yes! S-o-o-o-o-o-o wrong!*

Madison's eyes must have rolled all the way back into her head, because the next words out of Madhur's mouth were, "Um . . . Maddie, are you okay? Was the tandoori too hot or—"

"Huh?" Madison asked. "What?"

Madhur lowered her voice to a soft whisper. "Forget I said any of that, okay? I'm just being silly."

Madison nodded. But forget? She couldn't possibly.

Hadn't Madhur seen Madison and Hart holding hands at some point? Didn't she *know*? Didn't she *sense* it?

That night, after Madison returned home, Mom asked her about the big dinner. Madison told Mom all about the food and the orange door and the very cool Sri Ganesha statue. But she couldn't bear to admit out loud what Madhur had said about Hart.

The only one to whom Madison could admit the truth was her computer. She opened a new file before bed.

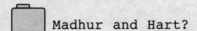 Madhur and Hart?

Just writing those two names together makes me feel all oogy. Wait. Is oogy a real word? I should have said something to Madhur about me & Hart, shouldn't I? But I looked over at her and my lips and tongue got stuck. Maybe it was the curry from dinner? It was like she shot me with a poison dart.

**Rude Awakening:** When is a sure thing not a sure thing? I'm not sure anymore.

Help.

Tonight I saw how exciting life is in Madhur's world. She has so much going on.

Sometimes, when she starts talking about Punjab and her family, I feel like plain cardboard. I have nothing going on; not like her. I barely even do the Web updates anymore. I haven't played my flute in weeks. I don't go to the animal clinic as often as I should (which is why I missed seeing those kittens one last time). If Madhur and I were in the same room, she would totally win the contest of who was more interesting.

I was never REALLY worried about Hart liking Ivy because after all, Poison Ivy is super fake. But Madhur isn't fake at all. She's the opposite of fake. And it's probably only a matter of time before Hart notices--REALLY notices--this fact. It's also only a matter of time before he realizes Madhur is way more interesting than me. Gulp. Then what? What am I supposed to do when things feel all shook up like this?

**Rude Awakening #2:** Life is just a fizzy bottle of Coke. One shake too many and then . . . PFFFFFFFFFFFT.

Wow. I hope _I'm_ not going to explode.

Can I do something to hang onto Hart-- before it's too late?

# Chapter 8

Phin woke Madison up extra early on Monday morning with wet doggy kisses on her nose and forehead. Even though she was up earlier than usual, Madison felt way less fizzy than she had the night before. She hadn't exploded—not even close.

Well, not yet, anyway.

As she dressed for school, Madison began to wonder if maybe she had been rushing things in her friendship with Madhur. After all, she'd been spending way more time with Madhur than with Aimee, Fiona, or Lindsay combined—and she felt a little guilty about that. Plus, what did she really know about her new friend? What if Madhur were just pretending to be like Madison—so she could *steal* Hart away? What if Madhur turned out to be like Ivy?

With time to spare before she left for school, Madison did what she always did when she had time: she went online. Usually, it calmed her nerves.

Much to her surprise, the in-box overflowed with mail. Madison went through and deleted all of the spam first, but there were many personal e-mails, too. Madison spotted three from Aimee (three?!); one each from Dan and Dad; and one from Fiona.

| FROM | SUBJECT |
|------|---------|
| ☒ BalletGrl | Mark the Date PLEEEZ |
| ☒ BalletGrl | & don't 4get |
| ☒ BalletGrl | 1 more thingie |
| ☒ Dantheman | thanx |
| ☒ JeffFinn | Dinner |
| ☒ Wetwinz | WUWC? |

Madison had to read the Aimee e-mails first. They seemed urgent coming one right after the other like that. And Madison hadn't said much to Aimee since the movies the day before. What could she possibly have to say that would fill that many messages?

From: BalletGrl
To: MadFinn
Subject: Mark the Date PLEEEZ
Date: Sun 27 Sept 10:12 PM
My bros r finally OFF the computer

so I can write 2nite. N e way I
wanted 2 say sorry about last wk. I
was thinking that somehow u were
still mad about it b/c u totally
blew me off @ the GNO movies and IK
you have been doing the project
w/Madhur these days but still. I
mean she's ok, nice, sure, but I
miss hanging w/you. OK I better go.

LYLASDA41S (heh heh, I made one up
is it lame?)

Bye 4 now,

Aim

Madison was surprised by Aimee's sort-of
apology. Aimee wasn't really good at saying she was
sorry, and really, Madison had been the one who had
done the blowing off, so if anyone should have apol-
ogized . . .

Madison hit DELETE and skipped to the next
e-mail. Aimee sounded different in this one.

From: BalletGrl
To: MadFinn
Subject: & don't 4get
Date: Sun 27 Sept 10:21 PM
OBTW IK u said u had a lot 2 do

w/the conference but u still said u
would go 2 my dance recital. I
wanted 2 say that the exact time of
the show next wkend is after 6 so
maybe yr mom can drive u there? I'm
a little nervous b/c I have TWO
solos (can u believe it) and b/c
Ben Buckley said he would come see
it. Whoa. Maybe he just said that 2
be nice 2 me. Well, I hope someone
comes.

Bye again,

Aim

And that wasn't the last Aimee e-mail. She obviously had a lot to say.

From: BalletGrl
To: MadFinn
Subject: 1 more thingie
Date: Sun 27 Sept 10:25 PM
_____
U borrowed my nubby green sweater
a while ago and well I need it back
now. Can u pls. bring it 2 school
Monday. Also, I think u have one of
my fave bracelets 2 that I loaned u
& I need that back 2. ok bye.

As Madison reread the last mail, her stomach

churned. After all, the green sweater and bracelet were loans from the *summer*, which felt like a million years ago. How could Aimee possibly need them back now? Was she being mean?

Madison couldn't bear to think anymore about it. She skimmed through the other e-mails.

Dan's note was just a thank-you for helping out at the clinic. Dad sent his e-thanks, too, for GNO, even though it had been overwhelming, with the arrival of the boys especially. Dad attached a page of bad jokes that he'd read in an airplane magazine. Madison had to laugh at all of them—even though they were really dumb.

Then came Fiona's solo message.

```
From: Wetwinz
To: MadFinn
Subject: WUWC?
Date: Sun 27 Sept 11:05 PM
```
It is wicked late but Mom said I could work on the computer n e way and besides I owe u an e-mail right? Well, it's a good excuse. OK so here's what's up: Chet is acting like the weirdest weirdo I have ever met. He started talking during dinner tonight (he never talks, just grunts) and he was asking me ALL these ?s about Madhur Singh. Ever since the movies Saturday

he's been obsessed. Does Madhur
like him b/c he seems 2 think that
she does? ok, I know I may be loony
here but I think we should fix
them up. Then maybe my bro will
just shut up.


LYLAS!

xoxo,

Fiona

p.s.: If he knew I was asking u
this he would KILL me so don't u
dare say n e thing.

p.s. again: Aimee called me earlier
and she is still mad about
Saturday, too. That GNO turned out
to be way dif. than the last one we
had, right? Is she ok?

Madison scanned Fiona's note a second time. She
thought again about everything that Madhur had
said the day before about boys. There was no inkling
of "like" for Chet, as far as Madison knew. Hart was
the one Madhur kept talking about. *Grrrrrr.* Chet
was perhaps the most annoying boy Madison had
ever known, but she felt bad for him and for herself

at the same time. Maybe if Madison let Madhur know the truth about Hart she would start liking Chet instead.

*This was getting so complicated.*

Madison glanced up at the clock. It was late! After rising early, she was now on the verge of missing homeroom. Quickly, Madison snapped the laptop shut without properly powering down. She pushed it into her orange bag along with two notebooks and a pencil case and jogged over to the closet to retrieve her jean jacket with the patches on the elbows.

"Where are you, Mom?" Madison called out from the center of the hallway. "I'm ready to go!"

Mom didn't respond at first, but then she came dashing down the stairs.

"I was in the shower; I was in the shower," Mom cried, hugging her bathrobe around her.

Phin danced his good-bye dance, too, around Madison's feet.

"I have a meeting for the conference after school, and then I might hang out with Madhur in the library to work on our . . ."

"Okay, honey bear," Mom interrupted sweetly. "Just don't forget to call."

"Okay," Madison agreed. She walked outside and headed straight for school.

After classes ended on Monday, Madison and the

other conference participants met in the auditorium. This was the day everyone had to submit their final topics of discussion. As the students walked into the room, Mrs. Wing handed out a more detailed conference agenda.

Dare to Be Aware!
Junior World Leaders Conference
Saturday, October 3
Far Hills Junior High

| 11 A.M. | Registration and Welcome |
|---|---|
| 12 P.M. | World Nations Luncheon |
| 1 P.M. | 7th Graders: My View of the World |
| 2 P.M. | 8th Graders: Assigned Country Discussion |
| 3 P.M. | 9th Graders: International Debate |
| 4 P.M. | Guest Speaker |
| 5 P.M. | Closing Remarks and Awards |

Madison's friends clustered together for the start of the meeting, taking seats in various rows on the left side of the room. As usual, Fiona and Chet caused a minor scene, fighting about something stupid. It wasn't too loud, but they kept poking one another and calling each other names, attracting the attention of at least one teacher. None of that would have mattered much if Madison and Madhur hadn't been sitting smack-dab between the two of them.

"You guys," Madison whispered to Chet and then Fiona, "I can't hear what Mrs. Wing is saying.

And you're going to get us all in trouble."

By then, a few kids had turned around to see what all the noise was, and they weren't staring at Fiona or Chet. For some reason, they were staring at *Madison*. Not only that, but Hart was at least five seats (miles, really) away from her when she needed him most. And Madison needed him—or someone—to rescue her.

Madison felt frustration brew inside her like water in a kettle that was about to go *shrieeeeeeeek*, so when Chet flicked his pen at Fiona's leg and hit Madison's knee instead, she stood right up with her arms in the air as if she were surrendering to the chaos.

The room went silent.

"Madison?" Mrs. Wing said.

Papers rustled as half the people in the room turned around in their seats.

"Gee," Mrs. Wing said to Mr. Gibbons and Mrs. Goode. "I've heard of enthusiastic volunteers, but this really takes the cake. Good for you, Madison."

"Volunteers?" Madison gulped. "I don't under—"

Before Madison could finish her thought, Mrs. Wing put her hands together and clapped. Other kids clapped, too, including Madhur, Hart, and Madison's other friends.

"What does she mean, 'volunteers'?" Madison whispered to Madhur. Her eyes darted from Madhur to Mrs. Wing and back to Madhur. "What did I just say . . . er . . . do?"

Madhur bit her lip. "Mrs. Wing asked who would help read the code of ethics at the start and end of the meeting."

"And I raised my hand?" Madison asked.

Madhur nodded.

*Oh, no.*

Throughout all of the back-and-forth between Chet and Fiona, somehow Madison had missed Mrs. Wing's request for volunteers from the class. So when Madison stood up all of a sudden . . .

"Speak to me after the meeting ends, will you, Madison? It's really not a lot of text to read. But it's an important job," Mrs. Wing said proudly. She was beaming. There was no way out of this one.

Madison leaned back in her chair and picked at a loose thread on the sleeve of her sweater. If she weren't careful, the whole sleeve would unravel. Of course, unraveling was a familiar feeling these days, Madison thought. She kept right on picking.

If Madison hated anything, *anything*, it was speaking in front of large groups. And now, this coming weekend, she would have to do it not once but twice? Her stomach flipped. And then it flopped.

*It's the end of the world as we know it. . . .*

"Are you okay?" Madhur asked softly. Madison hadn't spoken for a few moments. "Did you actually mean to volunteer? Because you didn't seem too happy, and you look a little clammy. Um . . . maybe you should tell Mrs. Wing that you made a mistake."

Madison nodded. "I know I *should*. But I can't."

"Why?"

"Because. You know. It would be too embarrassing to back out."

"Yeah," Madhur said. "I understand."

"You do?"

"You want to look good in front of everyone."

"As long as I don't throw up," Madison said.

"It won't be a big deal," Madhur said. "Really. You'll probably be great being an announcer. It's a very important job, and you're a very important person."

Madison moaned. "Yeah, that's me. Very important. With a very big mouth. Yikes."

Fiona caught Madison's eye from a few seats away. She made googly eyes, which got Madison laughing.

Then, Mr. Gibbons and a few other faculty members took over the meeting. They asked the students making presentations to pair up and practice. Mr. Gibbons and the other faculty advisers would be walking around the room to check on the kids' topics and outlines.

Madison turned to Madhur. "Oh, no!" she cried. "As if this meeting wasn't already enough like a pressure cooker! I thought we could just talk vaguely about our topic. But now . . ."

"Stay cool," Madhur said. "I have some notes we can use."

"Notes?" Madison said. "You know Mr. Gibbons.

He always wants details. That's how he is."

"I guess you're right. We can fake it."

"You mean *you* can fake it," Madison said.

"Yes. Leave it to me," Madhur replied confidently.

A few seats away, Fiona, Chet, Hart, Drew, Dan, and Egg all conferred with their own partners. It seemed to Madison that everyone was more prepared than she and Madhur. Why had they wasted all that time together gabbing and playing around— when they should have been studying? If they hadn't spent all that time eating tandoori and looking at photos, would they have been more prepared right now?

"So, here's what we should do," Madhur explained, pulling out a fat file folder of printouts. Madison gawked at the paper stack. She couldn't believe Madhur had done so much research—with so much backup material. All Madison had was a single page of barely legible notes.

"You did all this by yourself?" Madison asked with continued disbelief. "When?"

"I surfed the Internet last night for a few hours. You know, after we saw each other. I didn't want to be unprepared. I found some good stuff on poverty. Really good."

Madison glanced at the top page of the pile. She squinted to read all of the fine print. This *was* good stuff. It was super-smart stuff. Mrs. Wing would be very impressed.

> Poverty is the state of being without the necessities of daily living, often associated with need, hardship, and lack of resources across a wide range of circumstances.
>
> —*Wikipedia, The Free Encyclopedia*

As the two Maddies pored over the pages together and talked back and forth about the ideas they liked the most, Mrs. Wing poked her head into their "think" space.

"And how are you girls doing?" she asked gently.

Madison was tongue-tied. Madhur, however, knew exactly what to say.

"Doing fine, Mrs. Wing," she explained. "We have a lot of research on our topic."

"Care to share?" Mrs. Wing asked. She reached for the pile of material and quickly flipped through it. "Okay, this is a good start. But where is your outline?" she asked.

"Um . . . outline . . . yes, of course . . ." Madhur was close to stammering. Madison had never heard her new friend sound unsure . . . "Um . . . we . . . I mean, I . . ."

"I left the outline in *my* locker," Madison said. "Madhur has all of the backup material, but the specific outline isn't here. . . ."

"It's in your locker?" Mrs. Wing asked. Someone called to her from across the room. "Well, that's good. Just make sure you show it to me before the end of the week so I can review and comment before the conference, okay? And girls, from what I see of all this backup material, you may want to narrow your topic. You only have four minutes to present. Don't forget. Keep it streamlined."

"Of course," Madison said quickly. "We already took care of that. We have a really short and succinct speech. I swear."

"Absolutely," Madhur said, smiling.

"Yup," Madison added. She couldn't think of anything else to say. Luckily, Mrs. Wing nodded and walked away, distracted.

Madhur turned to Madison and let out a deep exhalation of relief. "You are my hero," she said.

Madison smiled. It was true. She had saved the day—at least partly. But this was no time to rest on her laurels.

"Hey, Finnster," Hart was there, squatting down in the row behind them. "Did Mrs. Wing like your outline?"

Before Madison could respond (to the question that was, in fact, addressed to *her*), Madhur started to reply. She talked about the close call with Mrs. Wing; and she talked about the reams of material she'd gathered on their topic (of course, presenting visual aids meant to impress Hart). Hart slid into a seat to listen. Madison watched helplessly, as if she were watching Ping-Pong. Madhur wouldn't shut up. She talked on and on and . . . why was she asking Hart about his topic—for the *tenth* time?

By now, the faculty advisers had made the rounds

of the auditorium. The room was dismissed. Hart and Madhur kept right on talking. They even laughed a little bit.

"What's so funny?" Madison asked, grabbing her orange bag from the floor.

Hart turned. "Maddie's funny," he said, pointing to Madhur.

Madison bristled when Hart referred to Madhur as "Maddie." He never called Madison that. No, she was stuck with "Finnster."

Madison was about to lose it when, at that exact moment, reinforcements arrived.

*Whew.*

Fiona slid into the seat next to Madison. And then Lindsay slid into a seat in front of them. Madison felt better. Now all she needed was a crowbar to pry Madhur away from Hart. Either that or she'd have to stand up on an auditorium chair and scream, "Hands off, he's mine!"

But she didn't do anything like that. Instead, Madison continued to watch silently as Hart and Madhur finished their conversation. Hart walked off in one direction; Madhur went the other way.

"Are you walking home?" Fiona asked Madison as they finally shuffled out of the room.

Madison shrugged. "Yeah, can we go together?"

"Of course. We do *everything* together," Fiona said with a smile, throwing her arm around Madison's shoulder. "BFFs, remember?"

# Chapter 9

<Bigwheels>: HELLOOOOO
<MadFinn>: OMG I'm so glad ur
  online r u @ school?
<Bigwheels>: I'm in my after school
  media lab on Tuesdays and u?
<MadFinn>: home after school
  <grrrrrr>
<Bigwheels>: so WTBD?
<MadFinn>: I feel soooo much bettr
  when we talk
<Bigwheels>: me 2 SO TALK
<MadFinn>: remember that new friend
  I told u about
<Bigwheels>: the one fm India
<MadFinn>: :>)

&lt;Bigwheels&gt;: so?

&lt;MadFinn&gt;: she likes Hart

&lt;Bigwheels&gt;: whaddya mean she LIKES him u mean LIKE LIKES him???

&lt;MadFinn&gt;: :>0000

&lt;Bigwheels&gt;: NO WAY wait she knows u guys r 2gether and she is liking him that is so lame SO SO LAME

&lt;MadFinn&gt;: hold up that's not it exactly

&lt;Bigwheels&gt;: ?

&lt;MadFinn&gt;: she doesn't know about him & me

&lt;Bigwheels&gt;: how is that possible? Didn't u tell her?

&lt;MadFinn&gt;: not exactly

&lt;Bigwheels&gt;: how can u be MAD then?

&lt;MadFinn&gt;: because my name is Madison that's how I can be MAD LOLOLOLOLOL

&lt;Bigwheels&gt;: seriously Maddie u can't be mad @ her if she doesn't know

&lt;MadFinn&gt;: she should be able to figure it out doncha think??? I mean Hart and I are always 2gether

&lt;Bigwheels&gt;: not really maddie b/c I'm a dork when it comes to that stuff I never notice who likes

who maybe she just thinks ur
friends
&lt;MadFinn&gt;: I guess ur right
&lt;Bigwheels&gt;: you have 2 tell her
when r u gonna tell her?
&lt;MadFinn&gt;: 2day she's coming over
for dinner so we can work on our
presentation 4 the conference
&lt;Bigwheels&gt;: when is that?
&lt;MadFinn&gt;: Sat.
&lt;Bigwheels&gt;: r u nervous
&lt;MadFinn&gt;: about the conf or telling
Madhur?
&lt;Bigwheels&gt;: BOTH
&lt;MadFinn&gt;: BOTH :&gt;0000
&lt;Bigwheels&gt;: wait stop. stop
freaking out its ok
&lt;MadFinn&gt;: NO what am I supposed 2
say 2 her?
&lt;Bigwheels&gt;: tell her the truth
&lt;MadFinn&gt;: that sounds like
something Mom would say
&lt;Bigwheels&gt;: yeah but it's tru
&lt;MadFinn&gt;: ok ok ur right as usual
&lt;Bigwheels&gt;: :&gt;) she'll understand
&lt;MadFinn&gt;: IDK
&lt;Bigwheels&gt;: she'll probably be
a little embarrassed that's
all

Madison stopped typing for a moment. She tried

to imagine how she would feel if she were in Madhur's shoes.

She wouldn't be a little embarrassed. She'd be drop-dead mortified.

Madison and Bigwheels talked a little bit more about music and movies and stuff but eventually signed off. Mom walked into Madison's bedroom to say it was getting late. Madhur would be coming over for supper soon.

Madison felt her cheeks flush pink. Panic started to set in. How could she possibly do this?

"I ordered some Thai food from that new place down the street," Mom said. "Your friend should like that, right?"

"Yeah," Madison mumbled. She wished Mom could cook up a big meal the way Mrs. Singh had done, instead of ordering takeout.

Mom sat down on the edge of Madison's bed. "Are you okay, honey bear? You look a little flushed."

"Just tired," Madison said.

"Come on," Mom insisted. She pushed the hair behind Madison's left ear and leaned in close. "I can tell when you're feeling down. You've been acting strangely for the past day or so. Talk to me."

"Really, it's just nerves," Madison said.

"Uh-huh. And . . ."

Madison could tell Mom didn't believe her. She'd better fess up.

"It's just . . ." Madison started to say. "Hart."

"Hart *Jones*?" Mom asked.

Madison nodded. "What other Hart is there, Mom?"

"I thought everything was good with Hart. After so much time spent worrying, the two of you finally decided to be friends. Well, you know what I mean. . . ." Mom said with a smile. "He is a good boy."

"Yeah, Mom. But then there's Madhur," Madison said. She tried keeping the words in, but as soon as she took a deep breath, everything came out in a rush. "Madhur told me she likes Hart, Mom. My Hart. And I just stood there like a bump on a log. I know I should have told her that I liked him, too. But I didn't. And now things are all mixed up. And I'm worried that Hart actually *will* like her more than me. And what if that happens? Then will I lose my crush and my new friend at the same time? And meanwhile, my other friends already think I'm acting weird because I've been blowing them off. Not a lot, but in little ways. And Aimee's worried because she isn't a part of our group like she used to be and . . . and . . ."

Madison sniffled loudly. Then the dam burst. She began to sob and threw herself onto the bed next to Mom.

Mom stroked the top of Madison's head.

"Oh, Maddie," she said comfortingly. "I knew something was up, but I had no idea you were *this* upset. Is this really about Hart?"

"Of course," Madison sniffled.

"I know he's a part of it. But what else is going on?"

Madison sighed and closed her eyes.

*Was there more to it?*

"I don't understand friends sometimes, Mom," Madison said with some relief. "What's happening with mine? People seem to change, and I feel like I just don't know why. . . ."

"Shhh," Mom said in a soothing, low voice. "Just take it slow. Okay? Now inhale and exhale a few times. That's good. Relax."

Madison felt her heart pound; she had gotten that worked up inside. But having Mom this close made things better. Mom wasn't around a lot of the time, and she didn't cook murgh tikka or anything fancy, but she knew how to make Madison feel better than anyone else could.

Mom always understood.

Madison rolled over onto her back. Looking up, she could see Mom's soft face. There were slight smudges of eyeliner at the corners of Mom's eyes and traces of plum-colored lipstick on her lips.

"Roowwwwooof!"

With just one *woof* as a warning, Phinnie jumped onto the bed and then onto Madison's chest. He licked her face in excitement and then tried to wrap his paws around her head.

"Phinnie!" Madison cried, trying hard not to laugh. "You're licking away all my tears."

"Rooooowoowowowoo!"

"Honey bear," Mom said, "Things will work themselves out."

"Please don't sound like a self-help show on TV, Mom," Madison said.

"Maddie, I don't like to see you feeling blue."

"Why does it matter so much what other people—or at least what my friends—think?" Madison asked.

"I know," Mom said, stroking Madison's head with her fingertips again. "You care so much. That's a very admirable quality, you know. I admire that about you."

"Thanks," Madison said. "But it doesn't help."

Mom glanced over at the clock in Madison's room. "It's nearly five. What time is Madhur supposed to show up?"

*Brrrrrrrrrrrrrrrrrring.*

"Wow! That's good timing," Madison said.

Phin let out another of his echoing howls, scooted down the stairs, and slid across the hallway to the door. Madison followed. When she opened the door, Mr. Singh was standing there with Madhur by his side.

"Hello," Madison said. Mom came over, too. "Won't you come in?" Mom offered.

*"Namaste,"* said Mr. Singh. "I have heard so many lovely things about you, and we had the great pleasure of having Madison at our home this weekend. *Dhanyavaad.*"

"No," Mom insisted. *"Dhanyavaad."*

Madison wished she knew what they were saying. Because of traveling all over the world for her job at Budge Films, Mom had a basic understanding of many languages, including Hindi. Madison guessed that that was what Mr. Singh must be speaking right now.

Mr. Singh and Mom never did step inside. They chatted politely on the porch steps. Madison led Madhur upstairs to her bedroom. Her orange laptop lay open on the bed. The cursor flashed where she'd ceased writing in one of her files.

"Holy cow," Madhur exclaimed when she saw the room. "This is amazing. Your room is, like, ten times the size of my room."

"Yeah, but it's not painted a cool color like your room," Madison joked.

Madhur walked around surveying the objects tacked onto Madison's bulletin board and spread out across the top of her dresser.

"This is such a great photo," Madhur said, admiring a picture of Aimee, Madison, Fiona, and Lindsay that had been taken in New York City. "I know I've said it a zillion times, but you have the nicest friends."

"I know," Madison said. "I'm lucky."

Madhur poked her nose into Madison's closet.

"All these outfits are yours?" she asked.

"Yeah," Madison said. "But it's not so many,

really. You should see Aimee's closet. She prides herself on her fashion sense—and her whopping collection of shoes."

"Aimee always looks just so," Madhur said. "I wish I had blond hair."

Madison grinned. "Mom ordered dinner. It should be here in a little while. You wanna talk about the presentation until it comes?"

"Good idea," Madhur said, flopping down onto the bed, nearly knocking the computer off the side.

"I was thinking about what Mrs. Wing said. About narrowing our topic," Madison said.

"Uh-huh," Madhur nodded.

"Maybe we should *change* our topic," Madison suggested.

"Change? Why?" Madhur asked.

"Well, when I read through the materials from the meeting, it said seventh graders are supposed to talk about something *personal*. The materials you got were more like a bunch of facts."

"A bunch of facts?" Madhur repeated. She seemed taken off guard, as if Madison had criticized her.

"I mean it in a good way. I mean, it's so impressive, all the detail. But I just wonder if . . ."

Madison felt something building inside. Unlike what she had felt earlier in the day, it wasn't fizzy or uncomfortable. She wasn't about to explode. Confidence was building inside of her—at last.

In her head, she heard Bigwheels's advice: *tell her the truth*.

"Madhur," Madison said. "I need to say something."

Madison felt her chest tighten a teeny bit with that sentence. She nervously tugged at the front of her shirt. *Could she bring up Hart at a time like this? Would there be another time?*

*Brrrrrrrrrrrrrrrrring.*

Madison jumped. The doorbell? It must be the Thai food, Madison thought. Then Mom called from downstairs.

"Maddie!" Mom cried. "Someone is here for you!"

Madhur looked askance at Madison. "Your secret admirer?" she joked.

Madison put her hands up to her cheeks and pretended to blush. "Me? Highly doubtful."

The two Maddies bounded down the stairs to the front hallway. When they arrived, the pair came face to face with three surprise visitors: Fiona, Chet, and Hart.

"Hey!" Fiona cheered when she saw Madison.

Madison noticed Chet's face light up when he saw Madhur there, too.

"What's up?" Madison asked.

"We were in the neighborhood," Hart said.

"Well, I was over at Chet's, and then Fiona said maybe we should come over."

"I figured we could play Trivial Pursuit or charades or something," Fiona said. "You finished all your homework on the project, right?"

"Not exactly," Madison said, shooting a look at Madhur.

Madison was momentarily distressed to see her new friend staring back—at Hart! Something had to be done.

"We're busy, right, Madhur?" Madison asked. When she got no reply, she turned to Fiona. "Um . . . where's Egg?" she asked.

"Home, I guess," Fiona said, her voice sounding unusually cool.

"They broke up," Chet said.

"Huh?" Madison asked. "You *did*?"

"We did *not* break anything," Fiona said. "Egg's just at home tonight." She flicked Chet in the back of the ear, and he winced.

That got Madhur's attention. She laughed. Madison saw that Chet was very embarrassed to be picked on by Fiona in front of a girl he liked.

*Brrrrrrrrrrrrrrrrrrrring.*

"Food delivery," Madison said. She stepped around Hart and the others to open the door.

"Hang on," Madison told the delivery man. "I need to get money."

For a brief moment, everyone just stood in the

117

hallway exchanging odd stares. Madison felt the tension. *Was Madhur still staring at Hart?* Chet was staring at Madhur. Who was Hart staring at?

"So, are you staying for dinner, too?" Madhur asked the group.

"Are we invited?" Chet quickly spoke up.

"No, dummy," Fiona said, flicking him even harder on the ear than the first time.

"Quit that," Chet snapped.

The twins bickered as Madison paid the delivery man and started to go into the kitchen with the food. Meanwhile, Madhur worked her way over to Hart. What were they talking about now?

Mom met up with Madison in the kitchen.

"I didn't know we were having a party," Mom said.

"It's not a party, Mom, it's a nightmare," Madison said.

"Now, Maddie," Mom reassured her, "it's not as dramatic as all that, is it?"

"I have to get back out there," Madison said in a whisper, "to check on Hart. He needs me."

Madison returned to the hallway. Hart, Fiona, and Chet stood there alone.

"Where's Madhur?" Madison asked.

"She just ran upstairs," Fiona said. "It was so weird. She said something about going home early. She forgot someone or something. I didn't really understand."

"Going *home*?" Madison asked, incredulous. She went to the stairs and called up. "Madhur?"

Just then, Madhur came down with her hair pinned up in a clip on top of her head. "I'm sorry, Maddie," Madhur said. "I don't feel well; I mean, I forgot; I mean, I need to go home right now. . . ."

"What happened? What's the matter?" Madison asked.

"I'll see you guys at school," Madhur mumbled, pulling on her jacket and heading for the door.

"At school? Do you have to go?" Chet pleaded.

"Yes, I have to go, now," Madhur insisted.

"See you around," Hart said.

Madhur didn't look him in the eye. "Bye," she muttered.

*Something was up.*

"You can't leave. We still have dinner—and all this work to do . . ." Madison said. "What about our project?"

Madhur seemed distracted. She asked to use the phone. Everyone stood there, not saying anything as Madhur dialed.

"My dad will be here in ten minutes," Madhur said, when she had hung up. "I really am sorry, Maddie, to rush off like this. We can talk in school . . . maybe."

"Maybe?" Madison replied, confused.

In exactly six minutes, Mr. Singh arrived. He seemed bewildered by the scene, too, but politely said his hellos and good-byes. Madhur left without another word.

Madison watched as her new friend got into the car. "Did we just enter the twilight zone?" she asked.

Chet shrugged.

"Weird," Hart said.

Madison turned to Fiona. "I need to talk to you," she said, grabbing Fiona's sleeve. They went into the adjoining room.

"What just *happened*?" Madison asked.

"Nothing," Fiona said. "I just was standing there, and she said something about Hart and I said something like, 'Yeah, don't Hart and Madison make a cute couple?'"

"You said that?"

Madison hung her head. Madhur had learned the truth. But unfortunately, the truth had come hard— hard like a rock.

And there wasn't anything anyone could do now to soften the blow.

# Chapter 10

All day on Tuesday, Madison worried about Madhur. She searched for her during lunchtime, but Chet said Madhur had not come to school that day. Of course, Chet would have noticed that. It wasn't as if he were a stalker or anything, but he already seemed to know her whereabouts. He was crushing hard.

Madison sent Madhur an e-mail, hoping that maybe *that* would be a good way to get in touch. It was easier sometimes to talk online than in person. But she had no luck finding Madhur in the real or the virtual world. *When was she coming back?*

That was when worry over the conference presentation set in. The conference was three days away, and neither Madison nor Madhur had *a)* provided

Mrs. Wing or any other faculty member with a proper outline, or *b)* planned the outline based on their "new" idea of writing a more personal story.

During Tuesday's computer class, a worried Madison began scribbling notes to herself. She hoped these would transform themselves into some kind of brilliant speech. In the margins of her notes, Madison absentmindedly doodled, too, as she often did: hearts, flowers, and names.

> Madison Francesca & Hart 4-Ever
> M & H = ((Heart))
> Madison Jones

"Whatcha writing?" Egg asked, interrupting her as he always did—just to be annoying. Drew stood beside him, snorting at Egg's lousy jokes.

"I'm writing something *private*," Madison barked, emphasizing the last word with a loud grunt. "Back off."

Egg reached for Madison's notebook, and Madison pushed him away.

"Hey!" Egg cried. "Mrs. Wing, Mrs. Wing . . ."

Madison buried her head in her hands. *Why was Egg doing this to her—today of all days?*

"Is there a problem, Walter?"

"No," Egg said, smirking. "I just thought I deleted something, but . . . I found it again."

As Mrs. Wing walked back to assist another

student, Madison huffed, "I'm going to delete *you*, Egg."

Egg and Drew just laughed and snorted.

"Since when can't you take a joke, Maddie? Lighten up," Egg teased.

Madison rolled her eyes. Of course, part of what Egg was saying was correct. She didn't have much of a sense of humor these days—especially not right now. But then again, how could she? There was nothing funny about standing in front of a Junior World Leaders Conference with no speech, was there?

*Gulp. Doom.*

"Egg, do you have your presentation ready for Saturday?" Madison asked nervously.

"Of course," Egg replied, full of bravado.

"Of course," Drew said, too. "But of course, we're cool, so what else would you expect from . . ."

"Arrrrrrgh."

Madison groaned. She couldn't listen or think so hard anymore. She walked over to Mrs. Wing, head hanging low.

"Mrs. Wing?" Madison mumbled. "Do you happen to know where my partner is today?"

"Madhur?" Mrs. Wing asked.

Madison nodded.

"She's out?" Mrs. Wing said. "Goodness, I had no idea. Which reminds me . . . you never gave me a copy of your conference outline. And I never gave

123

you a copy of the code I need you to read. My goodness, but we have a lot of work to do, don't we? And not a lot of time left to do it!"

"Don't remind me," Madison said under her breath.

"Oh, I'm sure we will be just fine, Madison," Mrs. Wing said gently. "You need to have more confidence in that fact. You always shine."

Madison forced a smile. Mrs. Wing handed her a copy of the ethics code to look over.

"Why don't we plan to meet here tomorrow, Wednesday, afternoon?" Mrs. Wing went on. "Just you, me, and Madhur. We can settle everything at once. That gives you a teeny bit more time to prepare. An extra night should do you good. Okay?"

"Okay," Madison sighed. What else could she say?

Mrs. Wing always understood about Madison and schoolwork, kind of the same way Mom did about personal stuff. An extra night was the bonus she needed. Madison could write up her own speech. Madhur could add whatever she wanted to it later— *if* she even showed up. And as far as the codes were concerned, Madison would just read those over and hope for the best. Although she hated standing up in front of crowds, she didn't have much choice now. There was no running away from her responsibilities, as much as she wished she could.

Before leaving school that night, Madison

stopped by Madhur's locker. She'd been working on a note.

Maddie One
    Please call me or find me at school on Wed. I need to talk to you ASAP about Sat. We have to do something FAST. Mrs. Wing wants to meet us in her computer lab Wed. after classes. I hope you can come. You have to come! And we have to talk, right? Are you OK?
              Your new friend,
              Maddie Two

Wednesday morning, Fiona told Madison that Madhur was back. She'd seen her at the lockers. Madison was relieved to hear that. It meant Madhur had seen the note. Or at least Madison hoped so.

After Madhur's absence the day before, as well as five unread e-mails (which Madison had marked *urgent*), and even a phone call, Madison had begun to wonder whether Madhur Singh had just dropped off the face of the earth. She'd come into Madison's circle of friends so quickly. Would she disappear just as quickly?

At the end of the day, Madison went to see

Mrs. Wing as scheduled. As she stood outside the classroom waiting to go in, she saw Mrs. Wing working at her desk, waiting for her and Madhur to arrive. She looked rather small, Madison thought, reclining in the large leather swivel chair. Her glasses were perched daintily on the tip of her nose as she wrote something in her agenda. A plaque on her desk read: CYBRARIAN AT WORK. Mrs. Wing was always at work.

"I'm here," Madison announced as she came into the computer room.

"Ready to talk?" Mrs. Wing asked.

Madison nodded. "I am," she said slowly. "But I have one little problem. You see, I haven't been able to find, well, I mean, talk to—"

Just as Madison was about to finish her sentence, Madhur raced into Mrs. Wing's classroom, loaded down with books and papers, in addition to the weighty backpack on her back.

"Sorry to be so late," Madhur said, her voice sounding hoarse. "I wasn't feeling well, so . . ."

"Glad you could make it," Mrs. Wing said reassuringly. "Now. Let's all have a seat and talk. We have a lot to do."

Madison said, "Hey," to Madhur, but Madhur just shrugged without really replying. Had one embarrassing moment really caused all of this drama—and silence?

"What do you have for me?" Mrs. Wing asked expectantly.

126

"It was really Madison's idea. . . ." Madhur started to say.

Madison was on the edge of her seat.

*Madison's idea? Huh? Where was this going?*

"Madison said we were going in the wrong direction with our original topic. . . ." Madhur continued.

Madison, fearing that Madhur's proclamations made her sound critical or negative, wanted to object.

But then Madhur said something *nice*.

"Of course, Madison is so right," she said. She produced a pack of papers from her pile. "I did all this research on poverty and the effects of it around the world and in the United States and most especially in my family's homeland of Pakistan, but then I started thinking about what *really* mattered to me. And it wasn't the topic we'd chosen. I was just spitting back a bunch of facts, like you said."

Madison was floored. What would Mrs. Wing think if she knew that all of this change had come from a confrontation between Madison and Madhur? Madison wanted Mrs. Wing to think that the two Maddies had their stories straight.

She glared at Madhur as if to say, *What are you saying? Please, just let me do the talking*. Madhur nodded, as if she understood everything Madison was thinking. "It was easier to write something for the conference when we cared about it personally," Madison said. "Of course, you told us that."

"No, no," Mrs. Wing insisted. "You two came

to this on your own. Like a true *team*. You found something that mattered. That's the whole point of the world leaders summit. We want to learn about and argue about things that really and truly matter. Sometimes that means taking the long route instead of a shortcut."

"Yeah," Madison and Madhur said at the exact same time. Then Madison spoke again. "We wrote a short piece together about the importance of bridging our own cultural differences."

"Hmmm," Mrs. Wing said, "tell me more."

"I think it's important for kids like us to know their roots, culture, and their *ma bohlee*," Madison went on, staring directly at Madhur.

"That's a person's mother language," Madhur added.

"Nice thinking, girls," Mrs. Wing said, nodding. "I am so eager to hear your presentation. You two seem to have worked very, very well together. It's good fortune that you were matched up, yes?"

Madison felt a knot inside. She wanted to blurt out, "Not really," but she said nothing; she just smiled and nodded back at her teacher and at Madhur.

"We know how lucky we are," Madhur added, sounding as though she meant it.

*Did she mean it?*

After a few moments, an impressed Mrs. Wing dismissed the girls and left to go to the teachers'

lounge. They packed up their bags in silence. Finally Madhur spoke.

"Thank you," Madhur said softly, "for covering for me. I appreciate that. I'm just sorry that I won't be able to do the conference on Saturday."

"Don't worry. It wasn't a big deal, I think—*wait.* . . . What did you say?" It took Madison a moment to digest the words. "What do you mean, you won't be able to do the conference on Saturday?"

"I would really like to go, but I just can't," Madhur said and shook her head sadly. "It sounds like you already have the perfect speech, so you don't need me anymore, anyway."

"What?" Madison didn't know how to respond. "I can't do the speech alone. We're in pairs for a reason."

Just then, Egg and Drew appeared at the door.

"Pssst! Maddie," Egg shouted from the doorway.

"Oh, Egg! What do *you* want?" Madison grumbled.

"Hart's looking for you," Egg said.

"He is?" Madison said. She turned to Madhur, whose gaze had shifted to the floor.

"Madhur, look . . ." Madison started to say.

But Madhur cut her off. "I'd better go," She blurted out before rushing out of Mrs. Wing's classroom in a flurry.

Madison stood back, stunned. She considered

racing after her new friend, but held back. She'd only known Madhur for a short time. How could these feelings be so real and so big? Why had the whole thing imploded? It couldn't just be about Hart—could it?

After lingering a moment, Madison grabbed her own bag and headed for the hallway. Madhur had vanished. Madison didn't have a clue as to where.

Slowly, she walked toward the girls' bathroom. With only a few moments before the next class, Madison needed time to calm down, breathe deep, and collect all her emotions.

Fortunately, there were no other girls inside the bathroom. Madison dumped her bag on the floor, leaned forward on the sink, and inhaled. The bathroom air smelled like sour antiseptic.

How could Madison attend—and do her presentation at—the conference all by herself? She couldn't. Could she?

*No. No. No.*

The door to the bathroom jangled, and Madison turned. Knowing her luck, Ivy and the drones would probably file inside. Quickly, she ducked into a stall. She peered out from beneath the door to spy on whoever entered the bathroom.

Madison immediately recognized a pair of turned-out ballerina feet walking to the sink.

"Aim!" she squealed, pushing open the stall door.

Aimee turned pale. She nearly collapsed backward against the sink.

"Oh. My. God," Aimee exclaimed. "You scared me stiff."

"Sorry," Madison said. "I didn't mean to do that. I was just so glad to see you."

"What are you doing in here? Don't you have a meeting with Madhur and Mrs. Wing, to work on the conference?"

Madison shook her head. "No. It's over."

"Over? What are you talking about?"

"Madhur quit."

"What?"

"She dropped out."

"No way."

"Yes, way."

"That's awful. What happened?" Aimee asked.

As Madison explained, Aimee nodded compassionately. Sometimes she could be moody or too focused on her dancing, but today—at that very moment—she was entirely focused on her BFF. As Madison talked and talked, Aimee was all ears.

"Okay," Aimee said, when Madison had finished telling her about what happened in Mrs. Wing's classroom. "Here's what you need to do: tell her what you're thinking."

It sounded a lot like Bigwheels's advice.

But it seemed next to impossible.

"You're kidding, right?" Madison said in disbelief.

"Look, Madhur's probably embarrassed because she was blabbing all that time about Hart and you didn't say anything, and now she's way too embarrassed to do the conference with you," Aimee said.

"You think?" Madison asked.

"Of course," Aimee said matter-of-factly. "And now you have to be the one to help her feel *less* embarrassed."

"Wait a minute," Madison said. "You don't even like Madhur. Now it sounds like you're taking her side."

"I *was* acting weird about her before," Aimee said. "But that was because I was jealous. Madhur is a very cool person. I see that. It just bugged me that you spent so much time with her, Maddie."

Madison couldn't believe that Aimee had come right out and admitted this.

"You know me," Aimee said honestly. "I like having you as my friend too much to let someone else come along and take you away."

"Take me away?" Madison asked. "What are you talking about? Where was I going?"

"For days you were spending all your time with Madhur," Aimee said. "I think Madhur's interesting. And I'd like to know her more. But that didn't stop me from feeling blown off. And then I had to drop out of the conference."

Madison didn't know what to think about this turn of events. It was as if all these feelings were flying around the room. She had to keep ducking so she wouldn't get slammed by them all.

"The point *is*," Aimee said, "you need to help Madhur feel better. Right? That's what friends do, right? You always make *me* feel better."

Nodding, Madison lunged and threw her arms around Aimee. "You're the best, Aim."

"Yeah, I know," Aimee said.

Madison felt a weight lift from her shoulders, even though she hadn't done the hard work yet. Could she resolve things with Madhur? Madison contemplated her next steps.

"So now I know what I have to do," Madison said. "How do I do it?"

"Write Madhur a note and put it in her locker," Aimee suggested. "Tell her you want to do the conference with her or you won't go. Say something like that. It'll make her feel a little guiltier about dropping out. I know that sounds mean, but I bet she goes for it. I would."

"I hope it works," Madison said. "I need her."

Aimee nodded. "And I need you to cheer me up, too."

"Why? What's wrong?" Madison asked.

"Dance."

"Dance is wrong? Why? You love it," Madison said.

"Yeah, of course. But I'm just way too nervous to think about my performance on Saturday, and the only people coming to see me are parents and grandparents, which is a bummer. None of you. I wish more of my friends could be there. But that wasn't meant to be a guilt trip. . . ."

"You're right," Madison said. "I should be going to your dance performance instead of doing this conference, shouldn't I? Oh, I'm so confused."

"You're doing the right thing going to the conference. You're good at that stuff. That is important."

"But you're important, too," Madison said.

Aimee smiled. "Just write the note to Madhur. Get her back as your partner. E me later to tell me what she says," she said.

Madison smiled. "Thanks, Aim. I feel better. Do you feel better?"

"Yeah," Aimee said. "A little."

"I'll let you know what happens," Madison promised.

"Cool," Aimee said with a flip of her braid. She twirled out of the bathroom, leaving Madison alone with her thoughts, a scrap of notepaper, and the beginnings of a note to Madhur.

Next stop: Madhur's locker.

Madison hoped that Aimee's idea would solve everything. She needed to get her conference partner back—and fast. Thanks to Aimee, she had a good plan that just might work.

# Chapter 11

 All Shook Up

One more day until the Junior World Leaders Conference, or FWLS (Fools) conference, as Chet has been calling it. He thinks the whole thing is pretty silly, which makes it absolutely clear that the only reason he's doing ANY of this is to get Madhur's attention. Though we all know now that she has her eye on someone else.

<Grrrrrrr>

Not that she's even coming tomorrow BUT I sure hope I see her today and everything is made better. Right now I have this crummy feeling inside and I wishwishwish I had said something about Hart from the beginning. I wish I hadn't pretended to go along with her when she admitted her crush on my crush. I was just so afraid of what she would say. I was afraid.

There. I said it. I was afraid.

So here I am sitting in homeroom before classes on Friday with one day before the conference happens, and all I can think to do is write in my files. Everything around me feels weird except the writing. Everyone's coming into the room and staring at me, too, like they always do when I'm working on this orange laptop.

I don't get it. I thought that by today I would be the happiest person at FHJH.

**Rude Awakening:** I'm on top of the world. But where do I go from here? Doesn't everyone know I'm afraid of heights?

Things with Madhur started out so new and exciting. And now everything seems REALLY all shook up and I'm not so high up after all and I am just SO not into falling.

<Double Grrrrrrr>


"Maddie," a voice said from across the room.

It was Poison Ivy Daly, looking as poisonous as ever. She took a seat next to Madison. Thankfully, the drones weren't around.

"Can I help you?" Madison quipped.

Ivy snarled. "Not likely," she said, crossing her

legs. Madison always wondered how she managed to balance on any stool or chair, in her itty-bitty skirt with her itty-bitty platform sneakers (that weren't really allowed in class anyway). But Ivy always did.

Class was about to start. Mr. Danehy clapped two erasers together to get everyone's attention. Mr. Danehy was one of the only teachers in the building who still liked to use his regular chalkboard.

Just then, static buzzed over the loudspeaker. Principal Bernard's voice blared into the classroom.

*"Your attention! Your attention, please,"* he said.

Everyone covered their ears, because whenever the principal spoke into a microphone over the loud-speaker, there was always a surge of loud, squeaky feedback.

*"Hello, classes seven, eight, and nine. Today is a special day. Everyone is anticipating tomorrow's big event, the World Leaders Junior Leaders Conference."*

Madison giggled because the principal had got-ten all the words mixed up.

Mr. Bernard cleared his throat. *"Here at Far Hills Junior High, we are proud to have several excep-tional students participating in Saturday's confer-ence. Your faculty advisers have told me that many of you have written excellent speeches and prepared great presentations. I cannot wait to see and hear all of you in action."*

Madison gulped. Hearing the conference spoken

about in such formal terms by the school principal made her nerves tingle.

"You're doing something for that dumb conference, aren't you?" Ivy asked snidely.

"Who wants to know?" Madison replied, just as snidely.

"Give me a break," Ivy said. "*I* want to know."

"I think the conference is a great chance to express opinions and learn new things about—" Madison said.

Ivy poked her finger into her mouth and pretended to throw up.

But Madison just smiled. She wasn't going to let the enemy get her down.

"Be that way. Fine," Madison said.

"Fine?" Ivy said. She started to laugh.

"Miss Daly!" Mr. Danehy barked from the front of the classroom. "What's so funny?"

Ivy blanched. "Nothing," she said, looking very, very embarrassed. One of the truly redeeming things about science class was the fact that Mr. Danehy often picked on Ivy. Unlike some of the other teachers in the school, Madison was certain that he saw through the enemy's veneer.

Madison stifled the impulse to laugh in Ivy's face.

Mr. Danehy invited the students to take out their textbooks. That was usually a hint—a sign, really—that he was thinking of giving a pop quiz before the period ended.

Madison groaned as she pulled out her book. The last thing she felt prepared to do was take any kind of quiz—especially not one in science. She hadn't done her reading assignments for the last two days. Now it seemed she would be quizzed on the very sixty pages she hadn't yet read.

Could this bleak day get any bleaker?

"I can't believe he's gonna give us a quiz," Madison muttered under her breath. "He gives us help by letting us review the chapters, and then, whammo! Here comes a quiz."

"Quiz? I don't *think* so," Ivy said. "Besides, even if we do have one, I'll just look at your paper for the answers."

Since the start of seventh grade, Madison and Ivy had been slotted into almost all of the same classes. And in *this* class, they had been made science-lab partners. Not only did Madison have to endure Ivy's presence, she had to endure it in the seat directly facing her own. Ivy always copied the homework and cheated on quizzes. No matter what Madison did to protect her answers, Ivy would find a way to steal them. She never seemed to study on her own.

"Ladies!" Mr. Danehy's voice boomed again. "Gentlemen! Let's keep the talk to a minimum, please."

Madison dropped her eyes. She didn't want to get called on by name in the middle of this class—or any class.

As she looked up, Madison caught Hart's glance. His eyes twinkled, and he grinned one of his *Hey, how are you doing?* grins. Next to him, Chet was grinning, too. Madison was astonished at the changes in Chet lately. It seemed as if ever since he'd developed his crush on Madhur, Chet had become cuter and way more likeable. He didn't make a joke out of everything.

*What did it all mean?*

"I think this whole conference is so-o-o lame," Ivy laughed. "For those of us who don't care, why should we have to put up with all this disruption?"

"Maybe you should just be quiet about it," Madison said, shooting Ivy a hard, cold stare.

Madison sat back on her stool. Had she really just snapped at Ivy like that? Somehow, talking back to the enemy got easier over time. Madison didn't feel as threatened or bullied as she had sometimes felt in fifth or sixth grade. Had Ivy lost a little of her power?

Hart sat there, still staring and smiling. Madison liked the attention. It was obvious why Madhur thought Hart was so cute and talented—and why Ivy still couldn't let go of her Hart fixation, either.

Hart was one of a kind.

*Madison's* kind.

With five minutes left of class, Mr. Danehy threw his hands into the air and said, "Okay, everyone, book bags away." He started to distribute quiz sheets around the class.

Madison turned to Ivy. "Good luck," she whispered sarcastically, and promptly covered her own quiz sheet, angling her body so there was no way Ivy could see even one of her answers.

Ivy looked steamed.

By the time the class bell rang, Madison answered all five pop quiz questions correctly. That gave her the jolt of confidence that she needed, leaving Ivy sitting there with a blank sheet of paper.

On the way out, Madison caught up with Hart.

"How did you do?" Hart asked. "I thought it was easy as pie for a Danehy quiz."

Madison nodded. "Yeah, considering I haven't done homework all week."

"You haven't?" Hart laughed. "What was Miss Ivy blabbing to you about during class?" he asked.

Madison bit her lip. "You," she said teasingly.

"Get out of here," Hart said. "Are you serious?"

"Kidding," Madison replied. "The truth is that Ivy was trying to copy my notes and my quiz. And she kept telling me that I was a big geek for doing the Junior World Leaders Conference. But we know the truth: she's the geek."

"Geek? Freak! What does she know about anything?" Hart said.

"Not much," Madison concurred.

As they walked into the corridor, Hart pressed the small of Madison's back, just to the left of the bag she'd slung over her shoulder. That caught Madison's attention, and she stopped short. "Hart," she asked cautiously. "Um . . . I was wondering . . . Did you ever say anything to Madhur to make her think that maybe she . . ."

"What?"

"Well, that maybe she was . . ."

Madison stalled. She wanted to ask if maybe Hart knew that Madhur liked him, or if maybe he'd said something that Madhur could have misconstrued.

"Maddie?" Hart said. "Is there a problem?"

*Not unless you consider being tongue-tied, jealous, and very confused a problem.*

"No . . ." Madison replied.

"Then what are you asking?"

Madison didn't know what to say now. So she didn't say anything. She slowly strolled away from Hart, right down the hallway.

"Finnster?" Hart called out, very confused himself. "Where are you going?"

Without turning back, Madison stuck up a hand and waved. She didn't want to see the bewildered expression on Hart's face.

"Finnster!" Hart called out once again, but Madison was gone.

She zoomed around the corner, past a few classrooms, through a pair of swinging doors, and through a cluster of kids talking in the hallway, past another bank of lockers crowded with students, and up a short flight of stairs. . . .

"Madison?" Madhur stood at the top. With a few more paces, Madison would have bumped into her.

Madison caught her breath. "I didn't see you," she said.

"Yeah, well, I saw you." Madhur said. "I saw you earlier today, too,"

"Oh?"

"But I didn't come over to talk," Madhur said. "Sorry."

"Oh."

"I should have said something. I know I've been avoiding you."

"Did you get my note?" Madison asked.

"Yeah, of course. I showed up at Mrs. Wing's, didn't I?"

"You did," Madison said. "But then you bolted again. We didn't really have a chance to talk."

"I know."

Madison was standing a few steps below the spot where Madhur stood; she climbed up so they could talk face to face. Then they turned and headed out of the stairwell and into the hallway near the lobby.

"I never should have backed out," Madhur admitted. "I do want to go to the conference, you know. I really do want to go."

"I figured," Madison said. "Then why did you tell me and Mrs. Wing the opposite?"

Madhur looked away. "I was too embarrassed

not to. These past couple of days I've been nothing but embarrassed. . . ."

"About what?" Madison asked. Of course, she thought she knew the reason—but she needed Madhur to say it out loud.

"You know why," Madhur said, staring right at Madison.

"I do?"

"You know."

"Yeah," Madison replied gently, remembering how Fiona had described the conversation at Madison's house. Maybe she didn't need Madhur to speak the exact words. Madison knew only too well what it felt like to be super embarrassed.

"You don't have to be ashamed on my account," Madison said, attempting to be comforting.

"Well, it isn't just you. I was embarrassed in front of *everyone*," Madhur said. "Why didn't you tell me about you and Hart?"

"Oh, that," Madison stammered. "I guess I got stuck. I felt weird. I assumed you knew. I didn't want you to be mad. I liked being your friend. I . . . don't know."

"Gee, that's a lot of reasons," Madhur said, smiling for the first time in a long time.

Madison nodded. "A lot," she agreed, smiling herself.

"How long do you think until my embarrassment wears off?" Madhur asked.

"Not long," Madison said.

"We make good partners," Madhur said. "Don't we?"

"We?"

"Me and *you*, of course," Madhur said, clarifying herself. "Who else would I be talking about?"

"Oh. Yeah, of course," Madison said. Even though she knew better, she thought Madhur had been speaking of Hart. "Do you think we can pull the presentation together in less than one day?"

"Of course we can. I'm glad you changed the presentation topic," Madhur said.

"It's both of our ideas," Madison said.

Kids moved past them, pushing and shoving their way to the stairwell and making their hurried way through the school lobby.

"Should we go somewhere else to talk about this?" Madhur asked.

Madison's face lit up. "I have a fantastic idea," she said, throwing her hand into the air. "You're gonna love this one."

"What?" Madhur asked, sounding very intrigued.

"It's Friday. We don't have school tomorrow. I bet you've already done your homework. "So, why don't you come over to my house after school? Bring your stuff. And then we'll do a sleepover. We can work on our presentation, talk, and go to the conference together tomorrow."

145

"Sleep over?" Madhur's eyes lit up. "Really? Just the two of us?"

"Just the two," Madison nodded. "Totally."

"But I told you that my parents don't allow me to do sleepovers."

"They'll make an exception if we tell them it's a practice session for the conference."

Madhur shrugged. "Maybe."

"Definitely!" Madison cried, trying to trump Madhur's doubtfulness with her own optimism.

"Maybe Mom and Dad will let me come, since it *is* you."

"I *know* they'll let you."

In the school lobby, members of the administration set up a tremendous cardboard display and attached posters to the walls and windows. Evidence of the conference was everywhere Madison looked. The conference was nearly there, and she was as determined as ever to make an impact—and solidify her new friendship at the same time.

Down the hall Madison and Madhur walked as they talked, arms linked together like a chain. They walked outside the school building and over to the pay phone under the parking-lot overpass. Madhur popped a quarter in and dialed her house for permission.

Meanwhile, Madison held her breath, crossed her fingers and her toes, and hoped for the very best.

# Chapter 12

Junior World Leaders

I'm trying to imagine myself as a junior
world leader. Yesterday, I would have
laughed milk out of my nose at the mere
notion. Today it seems more like it could
happen. In the past twenty-four hours, a
lot has changed.

Madhur's mom gave her permission for
Maddie to come to her very first-ever
sleepover at MY house. Mrs. Singh didn't
object one bit. In fact she said it was a
brilliant idea and she let Madhur come home
with me directly from school! I was

sosososo happy. The only person (or should
I say 'pooch') who had a small problem with
the whole arrangement was Phinnie. He acted
weirdly territorial all night. He kept
jumping in my lap to be petted when I
needed to do work. Eventually I felt bad
but Mom took him into her office and shut
the door. I hope pugs don't hold grudges.
LOL.

**Rude Awakening:** Why do they call it a
<u>sleep</u>over when you hardly get any sleep at
all? Madhur and I talked all night--about
school, about friends, and of course about
the presentation. Sleep was never in the
plan.

Random thing: I found out last night
that even though Madhur went to another
middle school before FHJH, she knew Ivy
Daly from camp and she ALSO had a bad
experience with Miss Poisonous. We have the
ultimate thing in common: a mutual enemy.
That meant trashing Ivy all night. I know
it's mean to talk badly about people, but I
couldn't help it with Madhur there, esp.
after how Ivy talked to me in science
class.

The only person Madhur didn't talk about
too much was Hart. That's cool. I had hoped
to clear the air and make sure that she
understood (*really* understood) that Hart
and I were a thing. But Madhur seemed way
too embarrassed to even say Hart's name. So
I'm not 100% sure if she's stopped liking

him. Am I worked up about nothing? I mean, Madhur's not going to turn around after all this bonding and come totally unglued, is she? That's the kind of thing only Poison Ivy would do.

This morning, we're bouncing off the walls. Conference time is really here. Madhur's mom dropped off clothes for Madhur to wear to the conference. She's got this purple dress and patent leather shoes that look a little bit like what I wore in fifth grade but they'll do. As usual, Madhur's dark hair will look sooo killer and she's sooo smart that it probably doesn't matter too much what she wears. When Mrs. Singh came by, she and Mom had a pot of tea. Mom is so good at understanding and interpreting different cultures and traditions. I envy that. She knows all the right things to do and say and ask. Did I inherit that trait?

Madhur is taking a shower while I type this. She says it takes her more than an hour to blow-dry her super thick hair. I'm the exact opposite. I get dressed in ten minutes.


Madison's computer pinged.

She clicked on the icon for her e-mailbox.

A new e-mail sat alongside a few others Madison had not seen the day before.

The newest one was from Aimee.

From: BalletGrl
To: MadFinn
Subject: DANCE
Date: Sat 3 Oct 6:46 AM

Maddie I think this is the earliest
I've gotten up on a Saturday in a
zillion yrs. I am so nervous about
the recital tonite. My mom, dad, &
two of my bros. are coming which is
the good news. My pal Sasha fm. Dance
camp is coming in fm. the city, too
which is way cool. So I <u>will</u> have at
least some friends there. :>) I am so
lucky 2 have the solo before the end
of the first act that is a BIG DEAL.
I know u & the guys have a reallybig
day 2day 2. I wish you oodles of luck
and all that. I wish I could be there
to cheer u on. I know u wish u could
be here 2. So that's ok that ur not.
ILYL&L as always.

Aim

Madison hit REPLY.

From: MadFinn
To: BalletGrl
Subject: Re: DANCE
Date: Sat 3 Oct 9:19 AM

It's early and YES I am online

150

and YES I got ur note. Thank
you. I hope ur toe shoes lift u
into the sky. Bye! I will call u
tonite.

Missing u,

xoxo, Maddie

After Aimee's mail, Madison clicked through
some other e-mails, from Gramma Helen (wishing
her good luck), Dad (wishing her more good luck),
and even Madison's uncle in Canada (who had heard
about the presentation and wanted to send his good
luck, too, even though he hardly ever wrote
Madison notes).

The very last e-mail in the in-box was from
Madison's keypal. With all of the excitement of
Madhur's sleepover, she'd missed it.

From: Bigwheels
To: MadFinn
Subject: GL
Date: Fri 2 Oct 9:12 PM
I am sitting here in our kitchen on
our family's new computer which has
a speedy DSL connection so now I
think I will be writing more often
(if that's possible). I have 2 go 2
dinner soon but I wanted to write

and check in. Is ur conference
tomorrow? I can't believe it. Can U?

Yours till the sugar cookies (I'm
eating one right now),

Vicki aka Bigwheels

p.s.: Wait! Did I say GL? Well, GL
times a zillion. That's enough good
luck for you and ALL ur friends.
Write back and tell me how it all
goes.

p.p.s.: What ever happened w/that
girl & Hart? U got the guy, right?

Just as Madison read the last line of Bigwheels's
e-mail, Madhur emerged from the bathroom, her
hair completely blown dry.

*That girl.*

"Do I look okay?" Madhur asked, patting the side
of her head. "Sorry to hog the bathroom forever."

"You look great," Madison said. She wasn't
going to say anything about the dress and shoes,
even though they weren't the most flattering fashion statements a seventh grader could make.

"That's a nice sweater," Madhur said, eagerly
pointing at Madison's ensemble. Madison wore a
purple cotton sweater with embroidery along the

neckline. She had paired it with a midlength black skirt, black stockings, and little ankle boots.

"Thanks," Madison said.

Together the two Maddies headed down to the kitchen for platefuls of pancakes and syrup, although neither girl was feeling particularly hungry. Nerves—and adrenaline—had kicked in at last.

Mom spouted compliments and encouragement throughout breakfast. She kept saying how proud she was to know that her daughter and her daughter's friend were taking their first big steps toward becoming powerful young women and leaders of the future.

"Someday you ladies will be running the show," Mom said.

"Don't go overboard," Madison said, feeling a little bit self-conscious.

When Mom stepped out of the room for a moment, Madhur turned to Madison. "Don't worry," she whispered. "My mom and dad would have said all the exact same stuff. Parents can be pretty exasperating with all their gushing. Doncha think?"

Madison giggled.

With a little time to spare, they put on their jackets. It was almost ten thirty in the morning—and time to get to school for the start of the conference.

Once Mom drove them to school, Madison and

Madhur were swept up in the wild energy of the place. A large banner hung outside the front door that read: DARE TO BE AWARE! Inside, Principal Bernard stood at the doorway to the school along with a committee of welcoming faculty and administrators. Teachers from other districts milled around, registering themselves and their students. The crowd seemed to grow exponentially in a matter of minutes. Madison spotted Fiona and Chet standing off to the side. She waved them over. The four started their own registration line.

"Why do we have to wait? I mean, this is our school," Chet grumbled.

"Yeah, well, we have to get our name tags one way or another," Fiona said. "Cool it."

"If I were any cooler, man, I'd be an iceberg," Chet quipped.

Egg, who stood nearby, let out a loud guffaw. Then Hart laughed, too. Soon everyone was enjoying the joke, including Madhur.

Madhur leaned over to Madison. "Maybe you were right. Chet is funny."

Madison was aghast. "Funny-looking," she quipped.

"That's not nice," Madhur said, nudging Madison. "He's cute."

"If you say so," Madison said.

"Finnster!"

Madison turned as Hart approached. He touched her arm. Out of the corner of her eye, Madison thought she saw Madhur squirm. Or was she being paranoid?

"Are you nervous? Are you nervous?" Hart asked Madison, gently shaking her shoulders.

"Well, I am now," she said, joking around.

Fiona leaned over and put her arm around Madison. "These two are gonna rock," she said.

"Definitely," Madhur said.

"Most definitely," Chet added, smiling at Madhur.

Madison wanted to smile, too. But she was too nervous, and not just because Hart said so. In exactly one hour, she would have double duty: in addition to her presentation with Madhur, she would have to stand up in front of the entire auditorium and recite twenty-five words. Glancing at the program, Madison Francesca Finn saw she was the sole seventh-grade representative for that part of the program.

*Yuck.*

Hart leaned in close on the other side of Madison. "You'll be great," he said sweetly, and Madison really, *really* wanted to believe him.

Just then, the rest of their friends appeared in the corridor: Lindsay, Dan, and Drew. Now the whole gang was there, buzzing about the conference along with everyone else.

Fiona crossed her arms and pretended to be mad at Egg. She'd been doing a lot of that lately. But within moments, they were walking side by side.

As they marched along, someone snapped a photo. The flashbulb lit up the area, and Madison turned and saw one of the school photographers, readying his camera for a second shot.

"Act natural," the photographer said, snapping a second picture—and then a third.

Egg threw his arms up and said, "Hurry! It's the paparazzi! Duck!"

Everyone giggled. Egg grabbed Drew, and they did duck, laughing, into the bathroom for a minute. After the two were chased out by a teacher who was inside, the group went into the auditorium and took their seats. Madison moved toward the front. She had one of the special seats reserved for solo presenters, near Mrs. Wing and the other speakers.

As she sat there, contemplating her twenty-five words, the entire week flashed before Madison's eyes. She thought about everything that had happened with Madhur and Hart and even Aimee. She wondered how Aimee was dealing with her own nerves about her dance performance.

Normally, Madison preferred being behind the scenes. She could hardly venture even onto an empty stage in an empty auditorium. But today Madison was being forced to break through many of her own barriers. Here was Madison, with a podium, a microphone, and hundreds of eyes staring back. This was a very big test.

Was she crazy? Could she do this? Would she pass out? There was no bell that would ring to save her this time, like that day in English class.

Something about the past weeks had strengthened Madison's inner resolve. Maybe it was the same thing the agenda sheet had said: she was daring to be aware. She'd made a new friend from a faraway place. She'd figured out that yes, she really did like Hart *that much.* And she developed confidence to speak out about her opinions and even to volunteer for something she would never have tried before. Okay, that had happened by accident, but it still mattered, didn't it?

Madison scanned the rows. She caught a glimpse of Hart, looking in her direction; he smiled.

Mrs. Wing leaned over and whispered in Madison's ear. "We're almost ready to start. Are you ready?"

"No!" Madison screamed inside her head. She felt her stomach do its usual flip-flop, but steadied herself.

"Ready," she replied meekly, and reached into her pocket for the file cards with the all-important words printed on them.

Mrs. Wing led Madison, along with the representatives from the other classes, to the front of the stage. Principal Bernard gave the welcoming remarks. Assistant Principal Goode followed up with some remarks about behavior at the school; then she introduced Mr. Gibbons and another faculty supervisor for the conference. At that, Mrs. Wing gently nudged Madison.

"This is your cue," Mrs. Wing said softly. "Listen close. We're next."

"Having a conference of this importance is something Far Hills Junior High is honored to do," Mr. Gibbons said. "And, as with model United Nations and other junior world leader events, there is a code of behavior and ethics that accompanies the procedural. We have selected representatives from the seventh, eighth, and ninth grades to explain these codes to us."

Madison's eyes darted out into the audience. For some reason it felt as if the floor had dropped away entirely beneath her feet. Was she sinking? Floating? Somehow she managed to wobble over to the podium with another gentle nudge from Mrs. Wing.

"Ahem," Madison cleared her throat.

Someone rushed over and quickly adjusted the microphone for her height. Madison looked down at her cards and then looked up again. She had survived making part of a speech in Mr. Gibbons's class. That had been more than twenty-five words. She could do this. Madison remembered a bad episode of an old TV show that she had seen once. On the show, one kid had told another kid to get rid of nervousness over public speaking by imagining the entire audience in its underwear.

Madison scanned the room again, but picturing

Principal Bernard in his boxer shorts only made her feel way *more* nervous.

She imagined Hart out there rooting for her, and Fiona, too. And maybe even Chet. And of course, Madhur, her partner. They had to be sending her positive vibes.

With that, she began to speak—her voice trembling.

"I promise to respect others. I will observe the proceedings with patience, understanding, and tolerance. Every individual is entitled to his or her own opinion."

Mrs. Wing clapped lightly, but Madison didn't move. She half expected to see Ivy out there, leering at her the way she'd done in science class only a day before. Was it over already?

The eighth grader who was speaking next came over and practically stepped on Madison's feet to get her out of the way. Mrs. Wing pulled Madison to the side of the stage and patted her back.

"Good job," Mrs. Wing whispered.

Madison breathed a huge sigh of relief and made her way back to her seat.

*One presentation down. One to go.*

After the remaining codes had been read and the conference was officially declared open, Madison twisted around in her front-row seat, eyes back on the crowd. It was lonely sitting there all by herself.

As some of the kids stood to mingle, Madison got

up and moved up through the aisle in search of Madhur. She thought she'd caught a glimpse of Madhur's black hair. But it was someone else. Where were Fiona, Chet, Dan, Egg—where was anyone? Not even Hart came into view.

Finally, at the auditorium doors, Madison saw Lindsay.

"Hey! Did you see the others?" Madison asked.

Lindsay shrugged as if she had some kind of secret she wasn't sharing. "The others?" Lindsay repeated cryptically. "What do you mean?"

Madison frowned. "You know what I mean," she said, moving past Lindsay and down the hall.

Up ahead, she saw a girl with long black hair. This time, she knew it was Madhur. She could tell by the hair clip.

But then Madison noticed a boy leaning close to Madhur. They were whispering. The boy was Hart.

Madison's stomach lurched.

*Hart? Again?*

The two of them were smiling and standing way, *way* too close to each other

Madison watched from a distance.

After all that had been said and done, how could Madison's new friend still pursue the guy Madison *like*-liked? They'd shared everything at the sleep-over.

What was Madison going to do now?

# Chapter 13

"Boo!"

Madison jumped and clutched at her chest.

Behind her, Fiona grabbed Madison's shoulders and jumped into the air in a twirl.

"Gotcha, huh?" she said with a grin. "I thought so. So, why are you standing here like a rock in the middle of the hallway?"

"What are you doing scaring me like that?" Madison asked, taking a deep breath. Just then, Chet, Dan, and Egg also walked toward her. Down the hall, Hart and Madhur turned around and headed in Madison's direction, too. They were all grinning, which made Madison suspicious.

*What was going on?*

"We have a surprise!" Egg cried as he came nearer. He handed Madison an oversize, bright orange envelope.

"What's *this*?" Madison asked. She smiled as she looked at the outside of the envelope. It said: *To Maddie 1 & Maddie 2.*

"It took forever to find an envelope in your favorite color," Fiona said.

"It's from all of us," Hart said cheerily, stuffing his hands into his pockets. Madison looked up at him, and his eyes sparkled back at her.

Was he thinking, "I like you, Maddie, I really like you"? She hoped so.

"What *is* this? Fiona, did you do this?" Madison asked.

"I can't take all the credit," Fiona said. "The whole thing was Aimee's idea."

"She's a really, really good friend," Madhur said. "But you know that already, right?"

"Aimee?" Madison pronounced her friend's name with disbelief and ripped open the envelope. Inside she found a brightly colored card. On the front was a picture of a lot of cows. All the cows were black and white except for one bright-pink cow. Inside, the card read: *You Are Outstanding in the Field (No Matter Where You Go).* The card had been signed by everyone, including Aimee. She'd written a little note, too, that read: *Break a leg and knock 'em dead. Love, Your BFF, Aim.*

"It's sort of a congratulations," Madhur said. "I mean, I don't know you very long, but your friends told me that you used to be really scared of standing up in front of large crowds. So today is a big accomplishment, right?"

Madison nodded. She couldn't believe her friends had done this—especially her one friend who wasn't even there. She felt a little like crying—but in a good way.

All at once, Assistant Principal Goode appeared. "Okay, students! Let's get a move on! On to the next part of the conference, please! Hustle, hustle!"

Other teachers crowded the halls, shooing students toward the cafeteria.

The first event on the day's agenda was an international luncheon. Madison wished Aimee *could* have been there for that. Aimee was the one friend who was game for tasting interesting foods—as long as no meat was involved.

Hart came up next to Madison as the group walked toward the lunchroom. Then, when no one else was looking, he tugged her arm and pulled her to the side.

"What are you doing?" Madison asked, almost tripping over her own feet. She watched as the rest of her friends kept right on walking down the hall. They didn't even seem to notice.

"I need to tell you something, and it can't wait anymore," Hart said.

Madison's heart pounded hard in her chest. She got a sinking feeling that Hart might be about to tell her something she didn't want to hear. Disappointing news? He'd been laughing with Madhur only moments before. This couldn't be good. Could she read his mind?

Hart pulled Madison through a set of swinging doors. They stood on the other side as the rest of the kids passed through. "Where are we going?" she asked. He looked so serious. Too serious.

"Hart? What is it?" Madison asked, bracing herself.

"I don't know how to say this," Hart said. "But I know I have to. And now is a weird time, I know, in the middle of school with everyone here, including teachers. I'll probably get into trouble for this for sure. . . ."

"What are you babbling about?" Madison asked, feeling impatient. She half expected that Mr. Gibbons or one of the other faculty advisers would walk through the doors and yell at them for being late to lunch.

"I just need you to—"

"What?" Madison cried. "We're going to get in trouble if you can't—"

Madison didn't have a chance to finish her next thought.

With one swift move, Hart grabbed both of Madison's hands in his hands. He leaned in and pressed close. Madison could feel his breath. Her mind whirred. Within milliseconds, Hart was closer than close—face to face—*right there*. Madison could actually smell his skin. It tickled.

"Finnster," Hart said softly, sweetly, *romantically* . . .

All at once, his lips pressed down . . . well, on her cheek. He'd been aiming for the lips, but missed. Nerves. Undeterred, Hart tried again, moving even closer this time. And this time, he made direct contact. There they were, lip to lip, hands locked. Like a couple in a romantic movie.

Madison's knees wobbled. She pulled away.

"Wait—" she said.

"Oh," Hart said, pulling away too. "Did I do something wrong?"

Madison realized that she must have had a shocked and bothered look on her face. But it wasn't that she didn't like the kiss. For some reason, all Madison could think about in that moment were chapped lips and stinky breath. Had Hart kissed the chapped part?

Maybe she wasn't a very good kisser. Would he want to kiss her again? Why was her head spinning so fast?

"Um . . . are you okay?" Hart asked.

Madison felt as if her tongue were made of lead. She couldn't even form the words to say, "Yeah, of course I'm okay. I'm *more* than okay."

165

She grabbed Hart's hands tightly.

"You kissed me." Words came out of her mouth at last. "You kissed me."

"Yeah, well . . ." Hart shrugged. "I thought maybe if I did it when you *really* didn't expect it—like at school—that maybe it would mean more. And then, when I saw you up onstage just now . . . I felt like it. More than ever."

"I don't know what to say," Madison said, blushing.

"I really like you, Finnster."

"I really like you, too."

"Okay. Um . . . we should go to lunch now," Hart said. "I guess if we stand here too long we really will get into trouble, and that would be bad. Besides, everyone's waiting for us."

Madison realized that they'd been standing there squeezing each other's hands for so long that they felt stuck together. But neither would let go first.

Pushing open the swinging doors, Madison and Hart saw that most of the other kids had made their way toward the cafeteria. So they hustled inside, too.

Their group took over the same orange lunch table they occupied every day in the back of the lunchroom. Madison walked up and took a seat next to Madhur, who smiled as if she knew somehow what had just happened.

"Pssst. Where were *you*?" Madhur whispered, eyeing Hart.

"Nowhere," Madison replied, feeling embarrassed

and more than a little self-conscious. Had kissing Hart left some kind of evidence that everyone could now see on her face—like fingerprints, except in the shape of lips?

Madhur grinned. "You're lucky."

Madison knew she was lucky indeed.

Everyone ate their share of the international food. They had Lebanese falafel balls with tahini sauce, Greek salad, Italian ziti, Finnish fish sticks, and other, assorted dining choices.

"Hey, not to get anyone nervous or anything, but we have our presentations in half an hour," Drew announced when everyone was done eating.

"I need another snack first," said Dan. He always needed a snack—even after a big lunch.

"I can't believe the time is finally here!" Madhur said aloud.

"You'll be the best," Chet said, smiling widely at Madhur.

"Thanks," Madhur said coyly. Madison guessed that maybe Madhur was starting to flirt with Chet after all. She'd definitely given up on Hart.

Madhur glanced back at Madison. "Should we practice one last time?"

They'd come so far in a very short time. Were they readier than ever for the big speech—or did they need another run-through?

"We don't need practice," Madison said confidently. "We can do this. I know we can."

Not all of the students were scheduled to present in the auditorium. The faculty had posted a list of teams who were set to appear in a variety of class-rooms. Madison and Madhur were assigned to talk on the second floor, in one of the math rooms. Fiona and the others were scattered around the rest of the building.

Madison and Mahur were third in line to present.

When their time arrived, Madison took the floor ahead of her partner. She tried to shake off any left-over jitters. Her voice cracked as she began.

"One of the most important things for us to remember about being a junior world leader is to understand others. In order to be a good leader, you need to listen. . . ."

She tried to stay focused, but her thoughts drifted.

*She had just been kissed—really and truly kissed—by Hart.*

"Um . . ." Madhur stepped in to finish that seg-ment of the speech. "Um . . . My own family speaks many languages at home, like Hindi and Urdu," she said.

Madison snapped back to attention.

"My family speaks English and sometimes doggy."

Everyone laughed. Madhur giggled, too, and went on. "Language and all talking are a way to connect and appreciate our cultures."

And so the two girls alternated for the next four minutes or so. Someone in the room videotaped the performance, which made Madison happy. She wanted to be able to share it with Mom and Dad. When they had finished, Mrs. Wing came over to congratulate them.

"Well done, girls," Mrs. Wing said, all grins. "I'm so very proud of you."

Madison felt a surge of emotion from her toes all the way up to the top of her head. She was proud of herself, too.

The girls sat back down and listened to the other five speeches. One pair discussed climate change, while another talked about AIDS. Another team talked about human rights, although their speech rambled. Each student brought a personal perspective to her speech. Madison was gladder than glad that she and Madhur had decided on such a personal topic. She knew it meant a lot in the context of the conference. She had a feeling that maybe—just maybe—their presentation had a chance to win some kind of conference recognition. She hoped so.

Throughout the next couple of hours, Madison, Madhur, and all the others bounced from classroom to classroom to observe the eighth and then ninth graders. Somewhere around three o'clock, a loud voice came over the loudspeaker.

"*Your attention, students,*" Principal Bernard's voice boomed. "*Unfortunately we have some bad*

news. *Our special guest speaker from the United Nations will not be able to join us today. Instead, we have moved up the closing remarks portion of the day to four o'clock. Please report to the main auditorium at that time. Thank you.* "

Madison checked her watch. Four o'clock instead of five? That meant that they'd be out of the building before four thirty.

It also meant something else—something incredibly important—something Madison had secretly hoped for . . .

*There would still be time to catch Aimee's dance performance! It started at six.*

Madison turned to Madhur, Hart, and the others. "You guys, I have a big idea," Madison said. She laid out a plan to get out of the FHJH building, onto a bus, and over to Aimee's dance studio. If they hustled, they could even catch Aimee's solo.

Fiona thought it was an excellent idea. But then Chet raised the issue of transportation.

"The school will never let us take the bus. They probably need our parents to pick us up before we can be dismissed. Isn't that how it works?" he asked.

"That is how it works," Lindsay said. "Bummer."

Madison hung her head. Chet was right.

"Wait!" Drew cried. "I have an idea. He pulled out his cell phone. Although cell phones weren't allowed in school, Saturday conferences seemed to be an occasion for bending some rules. Drew

170

mumbled something into his phone and then clicked it off. "We are too cool," he declared.

"What?" Madison asked.

"I just called my mother. I asked her if we could get a ride to the dance studio. She'll talk to Mrs. Goode and get permission to have us all leave at the same time."

"That's fantastic!" said Madhur.

Drew nodded. "I know."

"But your car can't hold us all," Madison said.

"We could sit on laps," Hart teased, nudging Madison.

Madison blushed again.

"Here's the good part," Drew went on. "Mom isn't bringing the SUV. She's sending the limousine."

"The limo?" Chet asked. "Man, are you for real?"

"Your parents have a limo?" Madhur said.

Madhur looked at Chet in disbelief, and the two of them started to laugh.

"There's only one teeny problem," Dan pointed out. "What if one of us wins an award? We'll miss the ceremony."

"Do the awards really matter?" Madison said. "Aimee is more important right now, right?"

"You're such a good friend," Madhur said with a grin. "It's the right thing to do."

Madison smiled.

About fifteen minutes later, a long stretch limo pulled up in front of the school. The driver popped out and directed Drew and all of his buddies into the back.

There seemed to be enough room for an entire hockey team back there; a panel on one side featured a television set, a mini fridge stocked with diet soda and juice, and even a stereo.

They all arrived at the dance studio in twenty minutes flat. Luckily, they were all dressed up for the conference, so they were well decked out for a special performance. Madison pulled a twenty-dollar bill from her pocket and bought everyone a ticket. It was her emergency money, given to her by Mom, which she kept stashed in a pocket in her orange bag.

If this wasn't the best kind of emergency, what was?

On the printed ballet program, Aimee Gillespie's name was featured prominently near a photo of her in a tutu, arms raised high in the air.

"Wow, Aimee looks good here," Egg said.

"Aimee always looks good," Madison said. She couldn't wait to see her friend perform. More than that, she couldn't wait to give Aimee an enormous hug and thank Aimee for the e-mail and then the card. Of course, Madison also needed to tell Aimee all about what had happened in the hallway with Hart—but that could wait until they were curled up on her sofa later, not in front of half the school.

The FHJH crew took up half a row of seats.

Madison and Hart were elbow to elbow on the left aisle. Madhur and Chet were paired off, too, Madison noticed. That was a good sign.

The friends waited patiently through four dancers' solos before Aimee appeared onstage in a gypsy costume, wrapped in gold and red scarves, hands poised and toes pointed. Aimee moved with precision and beauty. Madison was so happy to be there. She sat back, enjoying the show.

There would be plenty of time to revel in the success of their two presentations that day. There would be time to goddip, time to laugh, and time to to plan something for the friends (old *and* new) to do together. For once, maybe time was on Madison's side.

Of course, there would be plenty of time for something else, too: time to kiss Hart Jones again. And again.

Things were still all shook up.

But for once, Madison liked it that way.

## Mad Chat Words:

| | |
|---|---|
| ILYL&L | I love you lots & lots |
| MAM | Mad at me |
| GNO | Girls' night out |
| :{o} | Oh, noooo! |
| Sitch | Situation |
| WAYG2D? | What are you going to do? |
| <LMFO> | Laughing my face off |
| (((TAL))) | Thanks a lot—with a big hug |
| WUWC? | What's up with Chet? |
| LYLASDA41S | Love ya like a super-duper all-for-one sister |
| WTBD? | what's the big deal? |
| :>0000 | I'm freaking out |
| LOLOLOLOLOL | Lots of laughing out loud |

## Madison's Computer Tip

There are s-o-o-o many facts out there on the Internet. Madhur downloaded every last morsel of information she could find on our presentation topic. I thought that was smart. But it turns out that sometimes less is more. **Be picky about facts and figures that you pull off the Internet. Make sure to double-check and recheck all of your information against real sources.** Whenever I write a paper or do a research presentation, of course I go online to get help doing it. But I'll make sure I back up my facts and figures from at least three different, secure Web sites. Better than that, I think I'll run everything by Mr. Books, our librarian, next time.

For a complete Mad Chat dictionary and more about Madison Finn, visit Madison at www.lauradower.com